TO SHE

THANK YOU SO MUCH!

ALL THE BEST,

[signature] SEPT 2007

THE BIG DEAL

A NOVEL BY
HOWARD JENKINS

authorHOUSE®

AuthorHouse™
1663 Liberty Drive, Suite 200
Bloomington, IN 47403
www.authorhouse.com
Phone: 1-800-839-8640

First published by AuthorHouse 8/15/2007

ISBN: 978-1-4343-2395-8 (e)
ISBN: 978-1-4343-2393-4 (sc)
ISBN: 978-1-4343-2394-1 (hc)

Library of Congress Control Number: 2007905018

Printed in the United States of America
Bloomington, Indiana

This book is printed on acid-free paper.

Howard@HowardJenkins.com

www.howardjenkins.com

ACKNOWLEDGEMENTS

I am indebted to my many friends and family for their continued encouragement, positive feedback and well deserved criticism of my early drafts. And to Mary Linn Roby of A-1 Editing Service, a great author in her own right, corrected my many errors, kept me straight and on track. Particular thanks to my wife Lynda, for things that would fill several chapters on their own.

While this book is a complete and utter work of fiction filled with large doses of figments of my imagination, I'm grateful for a long and varied career that exposed me to many different and interesting individuals, some of which are blended into composites as some of the characters in this book.

PROLOGUE

HIS LIFE HAD become poker. All about poker. Knowing that the perspiration forming on his upper lip wouldn't be seen by the other players, he remained a study in patience and steadiness, waiting for the dealer. Paul kept his hands motionless, folded professionally in front of him. This game was the final qualifier for the tournament that would, he believed, set him free from his pressure-filled job and fill the emptiness that had formed in his life.

The game had moved up to $2,000 small blind and $4,000 big blind. In the next hour or so, to speed things up, the blinds would move to $4000/$8000 respectively. From the look at the chips stacked in front of them, Tommy G. had the current chip lead, Paul was second, and Patty and John had just a few hands left. It was just a matter of time for Patty and John. They both played nervously with their chips, stacking, shuffling, and reshuffling. He could not really count them out, because if you had a chip and a chair, you could still win it all.

Moving in his small blind, John counted out $4,000 and saw his stack nearly diminish. Each player picked up their two cards the dealer splayed about the table. Paul had jack and nine of diamonds. Patty grimaced and folded. Paul had a hunch she may have been playing too conservatively. The chip leader, Tommy, matched the big blind, "call." Paul called as well and John counted out the $4,000 big blind. Paul was looking at an unraised pot as the flop came out.

The first three cards of the flop: deuce, ace, queen of diamonds. Paul had a flush. Tommy, the chip leader might be slow playing pocket A's or Q's, trying to suck him in. Paul's flush could beat Tommy, unless Tommy flopped a set - meaning three of a kind, and then Tommy would be fishing for a boat – full house - to beat Paul's flopped flush. Paul went all in.

The dealer counted out the chips, making the raise to Tommy $36,500. Dakota John folded. Tommy stared at him, looking for something. Paul stared back, over his reading glasses. Tommy called and moved his $36,500 from his sizable stack into the pot. He showed his flush and Tommy G. revealed pocket deuces. Even with Tommy's set of deuces, Paul's flush had his odds to win at 4 to 1, with two cards yet to be revealed by the dealer. Paul tried hard to breathe normally and prayed silently that the dealer did not turn up a deuce, an ace, or a Q. Because if he did, he would be through. His hopes dashed to find another meaning for his life.

Thump, went the dealer's fist, burning the top card, and after what seemed like an hour-and-a-half, revealed a K of hearts. Whew! No damage! Thump, bury, reveal a seven of Clubs. Paul exhaled silently, raking in his sizable pot, as Tommy acknowledged. "Good Hand."

Soon, Paul would be on his way to Vegas for the finals!

CHAPTER 1

PAUL LANGLEY HATED sales meetings and disliked the sales staff. Because of the arrogant sales staff, he was running more than two hours late even though, as far as he was concerned, late was a relative term. Langley was a bachelor. Nobody and nothing was waiting at for him at home but his personal computer, which connected him to the world of Internet poker playing. Now, thanks to the long meeting, he wouldn't have as much time to play tonight, which he resented. Play on line had become very important to him. He loved the game because there was a core of emptiness in his life that it helped to fill. However, he determined not to think about that now.

The White BMW roared up the grade away from his job in Sacramento to his town home nestled in the foothills near Auburn, California, marking the end of a nearly one hour commute. He had spent most of that time thinking about the problems faced by the young company he had worked for for nearly four years.

eNovalon Software was a marketing and sales engine, but Paul was glad he was not in sales. Telling lies well, half-truths about their product and selling his soul to get a sale was not his bag. Software companies were all the same as far as he could tell. It was bad enough that in his job, as Vice President of Technical Services, he had to clean-up after, the overzealous, overpaid, lying sales force team that over sold the capability of eNovalon's products most of the time.

Although he had never finished college, Paul knew that, during his twenty-five year career, he had done pretty well for himself. A well-read, hard worker, he seemed to have a sense for business and office politics. A consummate negotiator, he was always looking for the win-win solution, with special skills when he came to retaining and analyzing statistics.

Perhaps, he thought it was his statistical analysis capabilities, that enhanced his poker playing ability since his experience in procurement and contract administration provided the opportunity to see business cases from both sides. Paul was at ease in almost every business situation, managing his subordinates as he wanted to be managed, fairly, consistent and graciously, without too much interference. He was also adept at striking up professional friendships with executives who had power to mentor and promote him, although he never thought of it as political maneuvering. It was simply how he was.

eNovalon was a software company that had been formed about a year before the founder and president, Gary Richmond had hired Paul to run the professional services department. Gary had developed and sold to the state of California a unique database software engine that had to keep track of millions of items in the huge and disparate warehouses, software that was now in its umpteenth iteration, having been successfully marketed outside government agencies. Because of the excellent sales and the skill of the marketing team Gary had put together, the financial future of eNovalon was bright indeed. In the meantime, Paul knew that he would just have to tolerate the sales team and do what he could to keep customers happy. Besides, he found, salespeople to be terrible poker players. Typically, they were always over-selling what they held, and underestimating the competition. Traits, that spelled disaster at the poker table.

He had been particularly glad to get the call from the eNovalon recruiter because he was anxious to get out of his last job in Rockford, Illinois and the fragile defense industry. Sacramento was not exactly a hotbed of software development and Gary had a difficult time recruiting good software developers and implementation staff out of Silicone Valley. But on his first interview trip, Paul had decided that Sacramento was not too bad. It was close to the Sierras, skiing, gambling, etc. and San Francisco was much less than a day's drive. Then, too, he had found an ideal place to live in a small, gated town house community in Auburn. During his first year or so at eNovalon, Paul had replaced nearly all of his older furniture and decorated his home with the finest furniture, appliances, and gadgets he could find. He was happy in his place, at least as happy as he had ever been. After all, he had no emotional encumbrances and that was what brought the problems. He was pretty certain now that good sex was about the best he could hope for.

Everyone at eNovalon knew of Paul's penchant for gambling and his frequent trips to Tahoe or Reno. In fact, Paul's qualifying for the well-publicized Hold 'em game in Vegas was big news around the office. However, no one knew about his more recent adventures into Internet Texas Hold'em playing.

The only good thing about the sales meeting today had been Maureen's presence. A very attractive woman in her mid-thirties who was supporting two children under the age of ten, Maureen was the manager of Inside Sales, responsible for all the paperwork that the sales team had to produce once they closed a deal and all of eNovalon's sales brochures. She had survived her recent divorce, in good part because Paul was a great sounding board.

Paul and Maureen had been good company for each other, both professionally and personally, since he joined the company. She had a great way of solving problems and bounced ideas off Paul frequently, particularly sales and implementation issues. And Paul had listened sympathetically to her as her marriage failed and she struggled through her divorce. He had harbored thoughts about her sexually, but had never pursued it - until now when, if he had he not learned his lesson over ten years ago, after having been caught fooling around in his office with his secretary, Sammie, he would have jumped now at the chance to meet Maureen in intimate circumstances. As for Maureen, she had jokingly suggested, during a meeting break today, that she would love to go to Reno or Tahoe on his next trip as long as he staked her to some gambling.

Paul had laughed it off but then had gone on to tell her that he really would like to have her company whereupon she surprised him with a husky, "Why Paul, I'd love to. Let me know the dates and I'll get my mother to watch the kids."

Paul had been about to respond with some suggested weekends, when they were interrupted with a call back to the meeting, although he had time to whisper, "Let's chat about this more later." on their way back into the conference room

The meeting had ended late and Maureen was summoned to a phone call that ended the opportunity to "close the deal," leaving Paul, disappointed that he could not strike while the iron was hot, so to speak.

The image of her swaying behind had stayed with him during most of his commute home while, at the same time, he reprimanded himself for going so far as to plan a weekend getaway with her. Not that that meant having sex. The rationalization amused him and he grinned, steering his powerful car past the gated entrance to his town house community.

Paul pushed the remote to open his garage door, and the big sedan slid into his spotless garage. As he wandered out to the mailbox to collect whatever junk delivery had come that day, his thoughts ranged back to fifteen years earlier when he had been a senior manager with an aircraft parts manufacturer in Southern California, responsible for internal manufacturing and offshore outsourcing, so busy grooming his career that he had ignored his wife Helen, telling himself that it was her fault because she had lost interest in sex within a few years of their ten-year marriage. Helen was originally a torrid affair that had got out of hand during his marriage to his first wife, Shasta. Their sex had been borderline kinky and exotic. Rarely needing foreplay, she was ready at the drop of a hat.

Paul had never been sure what had happened to her sex drive during the years that followed. Perhaps boredom had set in or perhaps she had been having an affair. All he knew for sure was that was what they had shared in the early years was something that might best be characterized as lust. Thank goodness there had been no kids from either marriage, which was an irony because the fact that Shasta was pregnant had been why they had been married in the first place. The point was, however, that it had all been unsatisfactory. Not one year had gone by without Paul being involved with someone else.

Fortunately, at least to Paul's thinking, after Shasta lost the baby the doctors told her that having another would be dangerous to her health. In addition, she had to stop taking birth control pills because of the potentially serious side affects. So after months of diaphragms and condoms and the times it scared-the-hell-out-of-them-when-her-period-would-be-a-little-late, Paul had decided on a vasectomy. After all, it was for Shasta's safety and peace of mind. And the freedom of being sperm-free suited Paul's life style to a T.

The women in Paul's life, particularly his wives, had displayed an interesting array of personal characteristics. First wife, Shasta, had been a perky blond with an athletic body, always up for playing tennis, able to light up a room with her energy while Helen, on the other hand, was a voluptuous, dark complexioned brunette with a brooding personality to match. Looking back, Paul could see that the little real emotional involvement he had had with either of his wives had been painful at worst and empty at best.

Since his last divorce, Paul had found dating fun, and challenging at the same time. Most of the women he continued to date, after the first one or two sexual encounters, turned out to be carrying what he considered too much emotional baggage, including but not exclusively confined to husbands, delusional ex-boyfriends, or children. Needless to say, he was still searching for Ms. Right, someone sexy, and intelligent, with better taste in music than an enthusiasm for the "top-forty," or God forbid, Country and Western.

For now, fantasizing about having sex with Maureen had helped get his bad day at eNovalon out of his mind. As he started to undress, his cell phone chimed.

Paul had resisted the temptation to get a Blackberry that would display e-mail, phone numbers, and a host of other bits and pieces of information as part of an attempt to remain marginally disconnected, but the numbers on the display looked vaguely familiar. It was Angela, director of training, presently on assignment in Indiana, teaching a client how to use eNovalon's software.

"God, I hope you can help me," She said. "Oh and I'm so sorry to call you at night. Did I get you at a bad time?"

Even as he assured her that she could contact him at anytime of the day or night, Paul found himself hoping that her problem would be something he could solve quickly. Poker called.

"I was supposed to get bug fixes today before my class," she told him, "but the IT folks can't get me connected to the server. I've left voice mails and sent e-mails and nothing has happened. If I don't get them tonight, tomorrow's class will be a disaster! It was bad enough today. Paul, can you stir up somebody, please?"

Promising to call her back within thirty minutes, Paul finally tracking down Al Gonzales, the VP of Information Technology, and told him what was wrong, adding that if he did not get the updates to Angela, heads would roll. In the meanwhile, there was time for a shower and a bite to eat before going on line.

Man, he had to loose a few pounds and get some exercise, Paul thought to himself as he looked at himself naked in the bathroom mirror. What was that old limerick? "Every morning it won't behave, standing up to watch me shave." Now it just hangs..." Hell. He'd forgotten the words. However, the point was that he was getting older. Furthermore, his job and addiction to poker were interfering with his sex life. It had been weeks since he had been laid or even masturbated.

Putting on his short terry cloth robe, he went to the kitchen to see what he could fix for dinner. As his Lean Cuisine was heating in the microwave, he uncorked a bottle of Riesling. Great wine and bad food. What a combination! Usually he did not drink alone, particularly before he played, but the day had been brutal.

By the time he had finished his dinner, the green display on the microwave clock said seven-forty-five, which gave him fifteen minutes before it was time to log onto the internet and playing some Texas Hold'em. As he sat on his patio, enjoying his first cigarette of the day, he contemplated his strategy for tonight, resolving not to fall into any duplicate patterns, to fold even he had something and to stick it to the other players when he had a chance. He was going to play $50/100, tonight which could mean large pots, and good practice for the big, no-limit Four Queens tournament in Vegas, less than a couple of months away now. All of which brought Maureen to mind. If he decided to go to Reno or Tahoe to warm-up for the Vegas tournament, it certainly wouldn't hurt for her to accompany him.

Paul had discovered Texas Hold'em watching tournaments on the Travel Channel. Hell, he had thought at the time, this would be easy. However, having found an Internet site and starting to play, he had discovered he was so wrong. In fact, his credit cards had crept up to their maximums during his indoctrination into this "easy" game. Paul thought he had better do some serious studying.

Realizing that he must spend some quality time learning nuances and odds, he had ordered several books on the subject including: Doyle Brunson's Super System: A course in Power Poker; David Slansky's Hold'em Poker for Advanced Players; Richard Herrick and Lou Krieger's Poker for Dummies.

He had also ordered several CD-ROM's, including Bob Wilson's Turbo Poker, all of which enabled him to hone his skills without it costing him an arm and a leg. However, using CD's and the Internet did not provide him with real people to practicing with, and left him unable to detect all the subtle physical signs that gave players away as they raised, called or bluffed, although he could work on never changing his own expression, no matter what.

As a consequence, for real practice, he had taken to heading up to Tahoe or Reno and play in $10/20 games, studying, odds, and trying to pick up "tells" from players while suppressing his own. Depending on his work schedule, he would take the pleasant two and half hour drive to Tahoe about once a month. Paul enjoyed driving to the Sierras as long as it wasn't snowing. Taking an assortment of audio CD's from his sizable collection with him, he would immerse himself in classical and jazz music.

Soon his Internet friends all recognized that when "BPL008," "Big Paul Langley – eight inches," logged on to their tables, they would have a run for it. Paul's long-term goal was to become good enough to quit his job, move to Las Vegas or Reno, and play poker for a living. He was well on his way, having over the last year or so paid off his credit card debts and amassed about twenty-five thousand in winnings, finally becoming eligible for the tournament finals by playing in many grueling sub-qualifying games in and around Tahoe and Reno. Now with the big tournament looming ahead, he could earn up to $100,000 or more. Paul's good salary and low expenses had already allowed him to accumulate a good savings for his retirement and several rainy days. This in spite of the fact that his divorce from Helen had cost him plenty.

Now, preparing to go on line, he wondered whether he was allowing poker to take up too much room in his life. During the day, he worked and during the night he played, but, hell, there was nothing to complain about, was there? He was his own man and that was, after all, despite a few nagging doubts, the important thing. He switched on the computer. Time to play.

CHAPTER 2

AFTER CHECKING HIS e-mail and scanning the several dozen entries in his inbox, Paul logged into casinoholdem.com to be greeted by a screen showing his $9000 cash balance, open tables, and game denominations. Paul scanned the open tables for the players he had come to know. He liked the $50/$100 no-limit tables as it kept most amateurs away. He could cash in some or all of the $9000 and receive a credit to his debit card, but thought he would wait until Vegas was closer. The entry fee into the Las Vegas tournament had cost him $10,000, but if he came in at least thirtieth, he would get his money back as he had that covered and more. Plus, Paul promised himself, he was going to have a good time in Vegas.

Logging on to table number eight, he found himself in the company of five other players, including, "TennTed," whom Paul had learned was a pretty good player, along with "MAC1," who never seemed to win big and some new ID's he didn't recognize. Clicking on seat number four, Paul waited for the next round to deal. The button had just left position four, so it would be a few hands before the ante and blinds got to him providing him with time enough to get a handle on the competition.

From the look at the chips stacked in front of the other players, it seemed that TennTed had the current chip lead, and that ViV069 was second by a large margin over MAC1, a Patty, and a Geoff. The latter two only had a few hands left.

Paul folded when his first two cards were an off-suited eight and nine. Watching MAC1 and TennTed being clobbered by a "ViV069," Paul clicked on the "whois" button to see if the player had filled out a profile.

Name: Vivian.

Age: MYOB.

Marital Status: MYOB.

Location: Rockford, Illinois.

Occupation: Financial Planner.

Years Playing Poker: 3+

Biggest Pot: $5500

Hobbies: Reading, Jazz, and Classical music.

Appearance:

Height and Weight: 5'8" – 145 lbs.

Color of Eyes and Hair: Green/Red

Vices: Smoke occasionally, drink socially and MYOB.

E-mail: ViV069@hotmail.com.

The similarities in his interests with that of the new player intrigued Paul. Not only did they share an interest in classical music and jazz, but she also lived in Rockford, his old stomping grounds where he had worked for several years before moving to California. Furthermore, he loved red heads with green eyes, and at 5'8 she was probably spectacular. True, she hadn't mentioned how old she was or if she was married which might only mean that she was a bit of a tease. But she had provided her e-mail address, which was all he needed.

Paul won a few pots over the next hour although action was slow, until he was dealt pocket aces. Paul had already blind raised the $100 as he watch all the other players call, except for Viv, who raised $250. Now this was going to a pot! Paul bumped it another $250 and every player called him. Viv did not re-raise him this time. Paul thought that might be a sign of weakness. Surely, she couldn't have pocket aces, too. Or could she? Four aces out on the deal? Not likely.

The flop revealed J of diamonds, ten of clubs, and the K of hearts. If somebody had pocket jacks or kings, Paul was in trouble unless the river had something. Instead of raising, Paul checked. The checks went around the table until Viv raised again, $250 this time. Damn, she must have caught a set! Paul gulped, and called along with every other player, only a bit relieved when the turn was an eight of clubs. His pair of aces was weak against several players who might have flopped a set.

The pot was nice, very nice indeed at over $3000. Paul started the checking again, sucking them in with slow play and everybody else checked, as well. Paul was sure he had them. Nobody apparently had a flopped set or they would be betting and raising like crazy. It seemed to him that only Viv had a chance with trip K's or J's and his pair of aces wouldn't outrank her. Here comes the river or "Fifth Street," five of clubs. No help to him, but the other players might have filled in a straight or at the least now flopped trips of their own. Paul wagered $500. It seemed forever before MAC1, TennTed, the others, and Viv all called. Damn! He hadn't scared anybody off. A very nice pot indeed, thought Paul. The computer turned over everybody's cards and a blinking W for winners appeared next to his and Vivian's names. She did have pocket aces and nobody flopped a set. Incredible.

Instant messages flew all around:

"Good Play."

"Four Aces, Damn!"

"VNH." Shorthand for Very Nice Hand.

"Way to be Viv and BP," etc. etc.

When Paul checked the time, he discovered that it was almost eleven, and time for him to turn in if he wanted to make work on time the next morning. But first, he decided to log off with his winnings, and then write an e-mail to Viv, congratulating her and commenting on the fact that they held aces simultaneously. No other questions, except to ask if the man in her life played. Not very subtle, but who cared. The lady interested him. Paul assumed she would check his profile, which would tell her that he was single and loved women. He also told her that he had worked in Rockford several years ago.

After having one more cigarette outside in the cool night air Paul turned in. His sleep was restless, disturbed by all kinds of crazy dreams involving cards and engagement rings, of all things. He awoke at four-thirty, an hour before the alarm was set to go off with a huge erection and an urgent need to pee.

Watching his erection diminish as he relieved himself, Paul tried to decide whether he should he go back to sleep or try to get some work done before his commute to his office. He had a busy day planned. Going to the kitchen, he punched his espresso machine on, and settling in front of his computer, logged onto his e-mail account.

When he saw a message from Viv069 in his inbox, Paul's heart skipped a beat.

Hi Paul:

It was so nice to receive your e-mail. You played very well last night too and thanks for the nice things you said about my playing. It was incredible that we both had pocket aces. I so enjoy playing Hold'em. Are you trying to qualify for the big tournament in Vegas in May? I have already qualified and am looking forward to playing in it. I did so well in the qualifying games, that my $10,000 entry fee was reduced to $2500. I sent it in last week and made my reservations at the Four Queens. I haven't been to Vegas in years.

No, there is no man around for now. I divorced over two years ago (second marriage, no children from either) and really like my single life again. John, my last ex, wasn't much fun and didn't like me to spend time on the

Internet. At my insistence, we would go to a local Indian Casino close to here, but John really didn't like gambling. In fact, as I now know, he didn't really like doing much at all. <Grin> Good thing we never had children.

How about you? I really like your profile too. I love big, er ah, I mean tall men - six ft six. Impressive. That part about loving women. Does that mean you can't make a commitment to one? <LOL> Even though you said you were divorced, you didn't mention any woman in your life right now.

I'll tell you my age if you tell me yours. I am 44. Let me guess you are at least that age or older…Hopefully, as I love older men.

I don't have to work tomorrow, so I was up much later than usual. I work in downtown Rockford as a financial planner. My usual time to play on Casinoholdem is early evening, probably before you get home from work out there.

Cheers,

Vivian.

Paul could not wait to hit the reply button. Beginning by telling her that he was forty-nine, with a birthday in a few months, he went on to say that he would be in Vegas for the finals and was excited about meeting her there. Paul admitted to the two failed marriages and several longer-term relationships and added there were no women in his life right now. Silently damning the sales staff for screwing up his personal life again, he mentioned he could not play tonight because he was co-hosting, with sales, a dinner for a potential client.

Before hitting send, he pondered what else he could add that would pique her interest. Since she had picked on his use of big, he might elaborate on the reference, as well as ask about the "69" as part of her ID. No! It was too early for any of that. After a minute, Paul added,

> *I've attached my picture and hope you'll send me one of you. I would love to see that red hair and those green eyes. Besides, I would like to put a face on a poker opponent with skill like yours.*

He attached a company head shot, one of those boring pictures businesses like to publish to make their executives look professional. Paul was one of the company's older employees, and their youngish president liked to show potential clients that there were some members of their firm suitably mature. With hair graying at the temples, a widow's peak, and laugh lines around his eyes, Paul looked the perfect part.

Paul's next day at eNovalon Software was as hectic as usual. One crisis followed another with the usual predictability and there were three more boring meetings about financial controls. An instructor, working for Angela, gave Paul a letter of resignation, with the result that Paul had to use all his executive skills, fatherly advice, and good listening ability to get him to take back. Angela would owe him big time when she got back from Indiana next week.

The bonus was that several of the meetings that day included Maureen with her great smile and personality. She had sent him an e-mail earlier, reminding him to be sure and let her know when he was going to Tahoe or Reno again, to which his short reply of, "probably in a couple of weeks," bought him some time. Their day was so busy that they didn't have time to pursue a private conversation and Maureen was not attending the waste-of-time, ass-licking, laugh-at-lame-jokes, meaningless-smiles, sales dinner tonight either. The only positive side of the meeting was that the company bankrolled dinner, a couple of martinis, and several bottles of wine. Also, Maureen's absence gave him the opportunity to remind himself not to mix screwing around with work!

After the sales dinner, Paul's BMW seemed to surge up the highway at 75MPH. Better slow down, he told himself, not that the two Martini's and a glass of wine with dinner would not raise the alcohol in his blood to a dangerous level, but he did not want to risk a hassle with an officer who might think differently. It was ten-forty-five. Too late to play poker, but maybe Viv had returned his e-mail. At the thought of her, the car seemed to speed up almost involuntarily.

As always, when he returning home, Paul found himself appreciating his decorator's good taste, particularly when it came to leather. After checking his mailbox, stripping off his clothes, and having his second cigarette of the day, he logged onto his computer. Good! His heart raced and his loins stirred. There was an e-mail from Viv:

> *Hi Paul. Thanks for the nice picture. You're a handsome devil! I've attached a shot of me and I hope you're not disappointed. It was taken a year ago or so at the beach in Santa Monica, when I was visiting my younger brother*

*and his family. That's me kneeling on the sand with my
little 4year-old nephew, Kerry.*

Paul clicked on the attached JPG file, which opened quickly,
thanks to his high-speed connection. Oh my! There was Viv,
kneeling on the sand with a little blond boy digging a hole in the
sand with another woman who, Paul assumed, was Viv's sister-in-
law. The surf was visible in the background, but Paul's eyes riveted
on the gorgeous redhead kneeling beside the child, her thighs spread
a bit, her ample breasts barely contained by her two-piece swimsuit.
Her sunglasses hid the color of her eyes, but her smile was radiant.
Paul imagined that cascading red hair spread over a pillow and
found himself wondering if it was her natural color as it had been
for Sammie, the sexy redhead he had employed some time ago in
California. But the important thing was that she was stunning. He
continued to read.

*I'm so excited that you're going to be in Vegas too. I
can't wait to meet you either. I did a Google on you on the
internet and learned you have had all sorts of "in-public"
life as an executive. I am impressed!*

Paul's career included making public speeches at affairs such as
trade shows and conventions, and he had even published a project
management paper that was currently running around on the
Internet. Flattered that she had spent some time doing research on
him, he read on.

Do you have any other pictures of yourself? It's very nice portrait, but I can't tell how tall you are. Remember I love tall men! If you don't have a picture handy, please take a digital, perhaps of you playing poker at your PC. Would love to have a picture of you that way. No. That won't give me a perspective on how tall you are. Oh well. Figure out something. I'll work on another one of me too. I'll borrow my boss's camera. She's good about lending me things.

I played a little tonight and beat MAC1 again. I think I wound up about $400 to the good. I lost a good hand early on with pocket K's. I had three of them on the flop, even though I didn't do anything on the turn or the river and JAL13 (whoever that is) produced a full house.

Paul, I just love playing poker and am excited that you share many of the same interests and tastes. What is your favorite symphony? Your favorite jazz artist? I love Mozart, but right now, I'm listening to Holst – Planets. I really like Oscar Peterson's jazz piano stylings too

All for now my handsome, tall friend

Vivian.

PS. Sheepish grin here. What do the letters and numbers in your ID mean? Just so you know about my "069," Casinoholdem assigned 070 to me when I first signed up, as they told me the basic Vivian was taken. So I opted for "069" and shortened it to Viv. I preferred being called Vivian. I like that number <blush> Is your middle name Paul? What's the "B" stand for?

She seemed too good to be true, Paul thought as he hurried through a bunch of company e-mails that he had neglected because of his busy day. Finding no crisis items, he hurried to respond to Vivian.

Vivian;

I can't tell you how thrilling your picture is. You are gorgeous! I'll take some pictures this weekend and send them off.

Mozart and Oscar Peterson? You have impressive tastes. They are on the top of my list, as well. My absolute favorite symphony is Shostakovich's Fifth, and I am partial to Big Band Jazz a la. Bill Holman, Stan Kenton, Johnny Richards, Gordon Goodwin, etc. I listened to a sexy version of some motion picture themes by Sax Goes to the Movies on my way home. I have an hour commute, I get to listen to my CD's a lot. I turn off my cell phone and just go with the music.

Tomorrow I'm going to ditch work a little early so I can play poker earlier than usual. I hope that you will be on-line then too.

My ID – "BPL008." Let's see, how can I explain this? <Blushing, modestly> My whole name is Paul Richard Langley. TPL for tall, didn't seem right. Let's just leave it at "B" and 8 are somewhat representative. You know what I mean? <grin>.

Hope this doesn't scare you off.

Hope to catch you at the on-line poker room tomorrow.
Have a great day.

Paul

He wondered if had gone to far with this e-mail, but hell, she'd started it. Life wasn't worth much if you didn't take a few chances, Paul thought, shutting down his computer. Sometimes he wished there was room in his life for a bit more risk taking. That, at least, would fill the gap in his life that nothing else seemed to be able to do.

CHAPTER 3

DRESSED IN FRESHLY pressed Levis, a Ralph Lauren polo shirt, and sporting his new New Balance sneakers, Paul arrived in the office for casual Friday to find that his office was becoming messy again. Post-it notes everywhere. More mail in his inbox. Several urgent letters had actually been placed on his chair. After starting his PC, he went to the break room, and poured himself a cup of coffee. As he was starting to return to his office Ted Jones, Director of Sales, smartly dressed, as always in a blue blazer and Chino slacks, stopped him and asked if he had heard about the disaster that was developing with ColdTech. It seemed that their president was alleging that eNovalon's software was not working as it was supposed to, according to the sale pitch, and was threatening to sue if it was not fixed ASAP.

"Shit!" Paul exclaimed, "You people sold him vaporware. You always expect my team to fix the gaps. Why don't you go yell at development?"

"I've talked to the development guys and the real fix won't come out for several weeks." Ted told him. "They have some work around ideas, but in the meantime you've got to help me save this account."

Back in his office, Paul gathered up all the correspondence on ColdTech, including the "Threat-to-sue." After reading it, he sent the following e-mail to his staff:

> *"All Hands" Meeting in the main conference room at 11:00 AM. Do not be late. We are going to discuss ColdTech - remedies, actions, assignments and anything else we can do to help. We're also going to spend some time on the general attitude around here, which in my opinion, has gone in the toilet.*
>
> *Paul.*

Returning to his voluminous e-mail inbox, he found that it included a "private" reply from Maureen about the Tahoe or Reno trip including the dates of some weekends when she could not get her mother to watch the kids. Hell, he thought, it would be hard to avoid taking her since she had weekends labeled yes or no, scheduled though the next two months. Even though Vivian was on the scene, he had to give the old college try.

Paul girded himself for the meeting, reviewing what he would say to his beleaguered staff. When it came time, ten members out of fifteen wandered in, the rest being away on business. Only Tom Z. was a minute late, which was, Paul thought, pretty good for him.

Leaning back in his chair, Paul assumed his usual "selling" posture, arms behind head.

"Folks," he began, "ColdTech is threatening to pull out of the implementation stage of the project and sue us if we don't get their project back on track. I know that Brett and his team are still there working through the problems, but we have to save this client. I'm open to any ideas short of taking a gun to the sales and development departments."

For an hour and a half, his staff came up with suggestions, some much better "work arounds" than the development folks had provided. Paul took copious notes on the broad white board at the front of the room and asked his right-hand-man, Dave, to copy and distribute them, concluding by praising his staff and agreeing to organize a team building off-site activity in the near future, perhaps after he came back from the tournament in Las Vegas.

Paul and his staff were not only well paid; they had stock options that could make them wealthy someday. After he reminded each of them of what their futures held for them financially, he grinned and said, "Right now we have to put our shoulder to the wheel, hold our feet to fire, keep our noses to the grindstone. Although come to think of it, it's hard to work in that position!"

They were all laughing as they filed out.

Paul finally left the office at four, not as early as he had hoped since, according to his calculations it was already six in Illinois. By the time he got home and logged on, it would be almost eight in Rockford. He hoped that Vivian would be on-line.

His inbox revealed that Vivian had read his mail, but there was no reply. Shit, he thought. I've scared her off with all that big talk business.

Logging on to Casinoholdem, Paul held his breath to see where Vivian might be playing and at what denomination. Using the "locate" button, he found her playing $20/40. Damn! Her table was full. Entering the same area, he was assigned seat six on a table at which there were no ID's he recognized. Paul was on the blind with his first hand, a suited three and four. Forty bucks in, he decided to see what the flop might bring. Garbage! Fold. Somebody won a small pot with trip kings.

As he waited for a decent hand, after folding four or five times in a row, an instant message popped up.

> *Viv069: Hi Paul. Nice to see you. Sorry my table is full right now but several players are almost out of chips. Any room at your table?*

> *BLP008: Hi Vivian. Nice to see you too. No room here, I'll try your table in a little bit. Did you get my e-mail?*

> *Viv069: Got your e-mail and all is great. You haven't scared me off… yet. <grin>*

Paul started to fashion a response, but before Paul could hit send, another IM appeared.

> *Viv069: Spot's open. Come and play.*

Paul played for a couple of hours, winning more than losing, but Vivian had him beaten by a couple of hundred bucks when she sent her next instant message.

Viv069: Paul, I'm tired. I'm going to cash in. I'll send you a note in the morning, probably well before you get up out there in Cal. Good luck tonight. You're playing well.

V

After flubbing a few hands and finding himself unable to concentrate, Paul decided to log off and go to bed so that he could concentrate on fantasizing about Vivian. Perhaps life was going to offer him something substantial for a change. He fell asleep with the picture of Vivian on the beach front and foremost on his mind.

Paul always had the same conflict on Saturday mornings. Go to the office and get caught up? Show his face to his hard working staff and have lunch in Sacramento? Bum around the house, playing poker. Watch an old movie or read a book? Head to the Indian casino? Finally opting to stay home, he fixed a bowl of Wheaties, drank two cups of espresso, and after putting some soft jazz on the CD player, settled into his computer chair. A shower and shave could come later.

An e-mail from Vivian was waiting for him.

Paul, (or should I say "Big" Paul? <grin>) sorry I didn't respond earlier, but I was busy, and after that I wanted to get to playing poker.

As I explained in my IM last night, you haven't scared me off. Not in the least. In fact, I'll tell you I'm thrilled about our having so many interests in common. You've come into my life (metaphorically speaking at least) at just the right time. There are real duds on Casinoholdem and the internet, and you are the first one that has really interested me.

I'm gong shopping with a girlfriend today (Saturday), then we're going to dinner and catch a movie, so I'm not sure when I might be home to play or, hopefully, see a picture of you in my inbox. Hint. Hint.

All the best and stay as sexy as you are.

Vivian.

Well damn, Paul thought, this was going well. All he needed was his digital camera. The thought of it reminded him of Kristy. She had been married with two kids, when he met her at the local Indian Casino shortly after he had moved to Sacramento and taken the job with ENovalon Software. Let's see, that was almost four years ago! She had been playing Keno next to him, and he hadn't been able help noticing how attractive and petite she was. Like him, she was playing Four Card Keno at a dollar a card. It drove Paul nuts to see her change numbers after almost every play since everything he had ever read told him not to switch until you won and maybe not even then, because the odds from the random number generator really didn't change. Keno was a difficult game anyway with huge odds stacked against players, but Paul did well enough to keep him interested, although poker was his first love.

Nursing a beer, Paul had offered to pay for her gin and tonic if she would pay for the next round. Her smile was sexy but he noticed the wedding ring on her finger. Play continued silently until, finally,

Paul leaned over and told her that she was losing so much because she changed numbers too often. Going on to explain that he had studied Keno probabilities extensively and that his subsequent experience with the game had confirmed the fact that he was right.

"Don't change numbers until you win," he told her. "There is no such thing as a pattern. The random number generator is just that - random!"

Taking his advice, she had played for several dozen more plays and then bam! Six out-of-six hit on one of her cards - $1600! She was so grateful that she had wanted to buy him a drink at the bar to celebrate. "After all," she told him, "you bought me a drink and gave me such great advice." And when he got up, "Oh, my God. You're so tall!"

At barely five feet, Kristy had had to crane her neck to look up at him.

Their second sexual meeting had occurred at Paul's town home, the first having taken place in a motel not far from the casino when Kristy could escape for an hour or two and they had gotten to know each other pretty well over the next three or four weeks. It turned out that her marriage was a disaster, and she was looking to get out of it, and move back to New Jersey with her two little girls, in order to be closer to her parents. Clearly, Kristy's' husband hadn't known how to treat her. Finally at a motel, they undressed and kissed that was when she put Paul's doubts to rest. "Jezz," Kristy had exclaimed just before her mouth slid around his rim, "my husband is big, but you're enormous.

Kristy had been a great deal of fun. When she arrived at his town home late one evening, she had pulled out her little digital camera.

"I'm going to take pictures of you, my big man; I want something to remind me of you other that just the feeling."

Paul had been a bit worried, about what might happen to the pictures later, but his ego would not let him dwell on it too much. After a round of great sex, during which they had posed and reset the camera many times, before going to his computer and uploading the nearly three dozen pictures to his hard drive. One shot, burned into his memory, was of Kristy facing the camera straddled over his erection and raising herself to expose most of his long shaft. She was a petite lady and the ease with which she took his considerable length still amazed him.

It still excited him to remember those moments, but he had erased the actual pictures some time ago, fearing someone would discover them after he was gone. Besides, they reminded him too vividly of his exhibitionist tendencies, going all the way back to his first marriage to Shasta, tendencies that he had sworn he would leave behind him. Paul equated exhibitionism with childishness and he tried to be mature within himself.

As for the next digital project, Paul, thought he would get out the tripod. He put on a clean shirt and took several pictures, wearing his granny reading glasses. Might as well be accurate, he mused. One of them looked okay to send to Vivian. How was he going to show his height?

After looking around a bit, he decided on the kitchen counter. He set the camera and snapped a few. Then impelled by a boldness that came on him unexpectedly, he shed his clothes and put on his short terrycloth robe. Snap. Snap.

Organizing the digital images, he picked a good one of him at the computer and a pretty good shot of him standing at the bar, robe open to the waist but covering his 'good parts,' at the same time hiding his modest love handles.

Attaching the two pictures of himself to an e-mail requesting Vivian to send a picture of her at her computer, he then began surfing through the scores of TV channels, finally settling on CNN headlines which featured a story about a runaway bride that had finally turned up in Nevada. Listening to her fiancé drone on about how much he loved her, Paul thought it was no wonder that she had run away. Clearly, the bozo didn't know how to fuck.

When he awoke from a one-hour nap, golf was over and an infomercial was blaring information about the superior qualities of what appeared to be some very sharp knives. Turning on his FM receiver to the local jazz station he slipped on a pair of shorts and flip-flops and click-clacked to the mailbox, stopping on the way to say hello to Mrs. Feldman next door before going back inside to sort out the mail which included a couple of bills, his Card Player magazine, and a letter from the Four Queens Hotel and Casino:

Dear Mr. Paul Langley;

Congratulations on qualifying for the Four Queen's first annual Big Stakes Texas Hold'em Poker Tournament. Confirmations for your hotel accommodations and tournament entry fee are included in this mailing. Also enclosed are the tournament rules, prize schedule, schedule of events and a release form for ESPN that must be returned in the return envelope by April 21, 2005.

Oh man, Paul thought it was going to be televised! His heart raced at the thought. The information included a schedule of events and an assortment of other information. In addition, the Four Queens had decided to make the entire tournament room nonsmoking.

Damn, Paul thought, poker playing was starting to lose its backroom charm.

The letter also contained a list of the tournament entrants qualified to date. Paul scanned the list to see if he recognized any other players. There were several name entrants, all of whom he had seen on television or read about, including several of the new, young guns: Joe Bartholdi, the sharpest player in the east; the Boyd brothers, who had been winning more that their share of tournaments lately; Dutch and Bobby, Scott Fischman, Tony Lazar, and others who were using this tournament to tune-up for the World Series of Poker which was scheduled for the Rio Hotel and Casino in late June. Vivian's name was there as well. Vivian Davis.

The prize schedule included first through thirtieth with a total payout of nearly two million dollars as well as a royal flush that paid ten thousand. There was a lengthy page about security and cash payout policies. It seemed that, for the probable purposes of hype, the Four Queens was going to put the two million out in cash for a limited time at the end of the tourney.

Paul put his head back on the soft leather of his recliner and thought about meeting a woman with whom he had so much in common. Not only did they share a love of poker but also it seemed clear to him by now that she was just the sort who could match him, move for move, in bed. After all, he had spent years perfecting his technique, one technique based on what nearly amounted to a clinical study of the many nuances of sexuality. Paul was blessed with above average endowment, but he learned that size does not matter. If you don't know how to use it and can't last long enough to satisfy your partner the size doesn't matter. But had never been certain until now that the women he had been with could completely appreciate it. And perhaps, just perhaps, this woman might provide him with more than he could even imagine.

CHAPTER 4

THE NEXT MORNING, Paul decided to jog around the neighborhood before breakfast. Checking the outside temperature on his weather station, he discovered that it was fifty degrees, not bad for this time year in the foothills. He put on his sweats, running shoes, loaded a Stan Kenton disk in his portable CD player, and headed out the door determined to get more exercise now that someone like Vivian had come into his life.

After his espresso, English muffin, and cigarette, he found an e-mail from her. She was thrilled with his picture and had attached one she had taken of herself that morning with the digital camera she had bought the day before. She went on to add that he was being a big tease keeping his robe closed for the picture.

Aha! Paul thought; *she really was interested!*

When he opened the attached picture, the only thing he could say was wow! There she was, sitting at her PC, grinning at a camera mounted high up over the monitor, grinning, red hair tied up with a sweatband. She had cleverly unbuttoned her blouse, and opened it to reveal most of her ample breasts, her left nipple, teasingly just out of sight, and the right one, half exposed. Paul felt the familiar stirring in his loins.

Okay. So it was going to be a hot exchange of pictures and e-mails. Paul was anxious to return a revealing picture, but wanted to shower and get ready first. During his shower, he got an erection that he soaped very well, but did not finish; time for that later, he thought. Right now he was eager to get the camera ready again.

Where to pose this time? Even though Vivian had hinted that she would like to see him naked, he wasn't ready to do that yet. Instead, he tried several poses with his robe open just enough to reveal some of the appendage in question. Finally selecting one that provided what was, in his opinion, the most enticing peek.

That night they met on-line at the same $50/100 table. Instant messages flew at first, so many in fact, they didn't play the first few hands.

> *ViV069: Oh, Paul, I love your picture! You big (no pun) tease.*

> *BPL008: Vivian, you have no idea what your picture did to me today, either. Wow!*

> *ViV069: Tell you what. If I give you my phone number, will you call me after our game tonight?*

The hold 'em game went to hell in a hand basket for Paul who, from that point on, couldn't concentrate on a damn thing, except calling her. Vivian, on the other hand, played flawlessly. After a couple of hours of Paul doing little more than treading water, Vivian IM'd him that she was getting off for now. Could he call in about ten minutes?

BPL008: *You got it. I'm playing terribly. Glad to end the misery.*

Paul carefully dialed Vivian's number on his portable phone and held his breath as the phone on the other end rang. How was she dressed? What would they talk about? How should he open?

"Hi, this is Vivian." The voice on the other end sounded as sexy as her pictures had looked.

"This is Paul, good evening Vivian. Good playing tonight."

"Oh Paul, thanks for calling. Well, you rather played well tonight, but a couple of bad flops got you. I know how that feels."

Their conversation lasted over an hour as they shared their personal histories, mostly concentrating, however on their mutual love of music, gambling, and poker.

Vivian had attended college for over three years and she was well on her way to getting a bachelor's degree in economics when she dropped out of the program to get married, after which she needed to find full-time work to assist her husband while he completed his postgraduate work in Geology. Later, after her divorce, although she never returned to college, she wcontinued to be interested in finance and economics, working as an administrative assistant in financial accounting and such. She had a good memory for facts and even appeared on Jeopardy once several years ago, coming in second. It occurred to Paul that she might come close to being Mrs. Right, although in the past, his hopes with a potential Mrs. Right had always been dashed with the later discovery of some baggage or other major mismatch.

Noting he had a cigarette during his pacing around during their conversation, Vivian mentioned the fact that she was trying to cut down on the number of cigarettes she smoked, Paul took a chance and told her that the one cigarette he could never give up was the one he always smoked after having sex. For a moment he was afraid that he introduced the subject of sex too quickly. But Vivian did not disappoint him.

"It's my favorite time to smoke, too," she said in an even huskier voice. "Relaxing after great sex. Problem is I haven't done much after sex smoking lately!" she added, laughing.

Paul was increasingly intrigued by this woman. She was open in a way that struck him as absolutely charming. Although he did not know her, he was becoming increasingly certain that he could say anything to her.

"Vivian," he said, "this is an age old internet chat question, but I'm dying to know what you're wearing."

"You first." She said and Paul could tell she was grinning, "You tell me, and then I'll tell you. Be truthful now."

"I'm stark naked as usual." Paul told her.

"Oh that's so exciting to hear," Her voice had a heavy, sexy quality. "Wasn't it cold outside having that cigarette? I suppose it's warm in California. Well, I'm not naked, but I am ready for bed. I have on silk Victoria Secret "baby dolls," pink and low cut."

Paul's loins stirred as he thought of her naked body next to him in bed.

"Wow! Sounds sexy,"He said, not bothering to hide his excitement. Clearly, Vivian was ready to play the game. "I've slept in the nude since I was a teenager. I love touching skin and it's wonderful when my partner is nude, as well."

"I'll bet you've had lots of partners in you life." Vivian's question and tone of voice, indicated, at least to him right now, she was one exciting lady. "Truth now Paul; how many lovers have you had in your life? Come on Paul, are there too many to add up?"

She certainly pulled no punches. Paul could count the number of women who had been as frank this on the fingers of one hand. She was smart, sexy, liked the same music as he. Was she being good to be true? He started feeling that this was the start of something really special, something he'd better be careful not to screw up.

"Well, let's see," he told her, actually stuttering, something he hadn't done since high school. He was used to women being coy which frequently made than less than truthful, but this one was grabbing him by the throat. "Two wives. Three live in relationships. And, maybe a dozen or so shorter time affairs. How about you?"

"A dozen or so, Paul? I like that 'or so.' I'm not quite that experienced. I lost my virginity to a seventeen-year-old high school senior when I was just fifteen. There were a couple of lovers in junior college. Then there were my two husbands, and a few affairs. Of course, that doesn't count a couple of one-night stands shortly after I left my first husband. And then last year...But that doesn't matter. When did you lose *your* virginity? How old were you? All the details please."

What was that about last year? Some hesitation on her part. He had been careful about guiding this conversation into sex and she was now taking the lead. Oh well, she was something all right.

Paul told her, with all he details he dare to include about the time when he had just turned sixteen and was visiting a fifteen-year-old girl babysitting in the neighborhood. They had become good friends during the summer, playing cards, and what not. She had called him to tell him that the two little kids she was watching were finally asleep and in spite of the parents' warning about having anybody over asked him to come over and watch TV with her. Sitting on the couch together, she placed her hand on his leg and told him she had seen him naked through Paul's bedroom window when she was visiting next door. She asked if she could see "it" now, up close. Paul had obliged her, and before long, they were on the floor trying to have sex. When, he finally got it in, oh, she began moaning so loud that he was afraid she would wake the kids. He had pulled out before he came because he was so concerned about her getting pregnant. After which she gave Paul a hand job.

"That's it," Paul concluded, "It was pretty exciting for a sixteen-year-old boy though. I masturbated twice a day for weeks after that thinking about it."

"Oh Paul, that sounds like my first time too," Vivian said breathlessly, "but he did come inside me. I know he wasn't as big as you are. In fact, he was smaller than some of my later lovers. I never had that breaking cherry pain that everybody talked about, but I was so worried about getting pregnant that I couldn't sleep for weeks until my period finally came. Turns out, I didn't have anything to worry about, because I can't ever have children. Oh well. Here's to great sex."

Paul decided to go for broke. After all, he told himself, she had started it. "What is your favorite sexual position?" He asked her, and then damned himself for taking the chance of offending her.

After all, she had just brought the subject to a sort of conclusion by pretending to toast great sex.

"I like every position," She said finally after what seemed like an eternity. "I guess if I had to choose, I'd be on top, but I love it all ways. Doggie style sometimes, because of the feeling of a different kind of pressure. But, Paul, you're so big, I might not manage it that way. And then there's your height. You're almost a foot taller than me."

Suddenly Paul was aware that he was feeling a sense of freedom that he had thought was lost forever. A sense of bonding and intimacy with this woman that he hadn't felt in years or at all. She was exciting, and he reminded himself again, don't screw this up!

When the conversation turned from sex to the trip to Vegas, it was Vivian who suggested that they save some expenses by sharing a room. If there was something Vivian wasn't, it was bashful. This was moving a bit fast even for Paul. By the time they got around to talking about poker, his erection had long since subsided.

"My reservation and entry forms came in the mail today," Vivian told him, "I'm so excited!"

Paul told her his entry forms had arrived today, too, and that he was a bit surprised to discover that the finals, at least, would be televised and it might be a little intimidating to let the entire country see one's pocket cards. Vivian reminded him that that was something they might not have to worry about since they might not make the last table. Oddly enough, the idea that that was a possibility annoyed Paul. He was an extraordinary player and so was she. Neither of them should sell the other short.

Vivian recalled their first game together when they both had pocket aces. "Too bad we weren't talking on the phone when we had those aces," she said. "We could have sucked the entire table in after the flop."

If she had sounded like a sexpot earlier, she was, Paul noted, all business now. "But we didn't know if somebody had flopped a set, as I recall." Paul reminded her. "Knowing we both had a pair of aces wouldn't have changed much."

"True," Vivian replied, "But what if we both had pocket pairs and flopped a set. We could have wiped them all out, knowing one of us would be the likely winner. We could have shared the pot."

Although Paul wasn't sure he liked where this was going, he was intrigued. "I've always suspected players at internet tables could be communicating about each other's hands," he admitted, "but the truth is, if you play intelligently, they still don't know what *you* have. I'm not sure it's worth it in these small internet games."

But Vivian would not let up. "What about a big, big game, Paul?" She demanded, her voice edgier now. "Let us say we're at the final table together in Vegas, and we figure out how to tell each other what we have in the pocket. We could improve the odds considerably."

Paul had to admit that thinking about cheating was fun, but he was sure he wouldn't really do it. Vivian was certainly a free spirit and her comments had him wondering about her now. Was she testing him? Would this kind of thinking and daring be dangerous to her? If he let her run with this idea, she could be perilous to him and worse, to herself. He'd just have to go slow and be careful how he handled this strange and surprising side of her.

"It might be easy to come up with a good communication scheme, but I'd be concerned about the security cameras picking it up," Paul reminded her. "I'm pretty sure those casino security experts would figure us out, never mind the other players."

"Well, its fun thinking about." Vivian said as if the wind had suddenly been taken out of her sails.

"I'd rather plot a robbery," Paul said, trying to lighten the mood and see if this side of her was serious or just testing him.

Planning a robbery. The excitement that it could bring to his life. Although Vivian seemed to worth taking these risks as she stirred him in a different way and wasn't just sex. No. He couldn't possibly cheat or steal. Could he?

After their final "good nights, Paul stared at the phone not sure what to think. Clearly this woman could be a lot of trouble, but exciting. It was, he reminded himself, too early to tell. After all, she didn't know him either. They'd just have to see how this developed. The only regret he had about their conversation was that bit about how easily they might be able to cheat. And then he had mentioned robbery. What had he been thinking?

Paul had always been fascinated by "caper" movies, *Oceans 11*, *Thomas Crowne Affair*, *Italian Job*, *Lady Killers*, and the likes. Even though Paul was well off, he still often thought about the big heist, a safe one, although he had never came up with a good plot that wasn't too risky or involved a situation he did not know enough about like casino or bank security systems. Theft, or a grand scheme, had been only a fantasy lurking in the back of his mind. Until this unknown woman at the other end of the Internet had awakened that and a good many other fantasies, as well.

CHAPTER 5

THE NEXT DAY at the office was actually calmer than usual. The Cold Tech situation was well in hand and Angela's classes in Indiana were now going very well. Paul fussed with the controller's new spreadsheet requirement for the balance of the fiscal year's budget and met with his staff on an individual basis to go over staffing and expense requirements, as well as having lunch with Al Gonzales, the VP of Information Technology to discuss new infrastructure requirements and Al's commitment to support Paul and his team. Al was one of the lesser stars Gary had had to settle for when recruiting better candidates to Sacramento in the Information Technology field had proven difficult.

Al droned on about servers and broadband and at some time Paul's mind wandered off to thoughts about Maureen, who was not in today, Vivian and poker, in that order. Al's presence reminded him that he really did not have very close male friends. Never had. For Paul, men seemed to be disingenuous. Always competing, trying to out do each other, egos getting in the way of honesty. It also seemed to Paul, many men didn't know the first thing about how to treat women. He'd seen it so often in women he'd known that their boyfriends and husbands failed to show respect and treat their ladies as equals. Paul had always enjoyed the company of women over men. Sure, he had some men friends to play golf, poker and occasional bar carousing, but that was rare. And he certainly never shared intimate secrets with men, only with women.

Later, when he arrived home, it was evident that Maria had been there and performed her usual great job. All of his dirty clothes were washed, ironed, and hung in his large master walk-in closet. "Thank you for the check Mr. Paul,' her note said. "Be back next Monday."

The refrigerator stared back at Paul as he looked inside trying to decide what to prepare for dinner. There was nothing much left and what there was didn't look particularly appetizing even though he was hungry. When he got home from grocery shopping, a call from Vivian was waiting for him.

Paul punched it up and heard Vivian's voice, set in its sultriest mode. It was extraordinary that this woman was giving his life a much needed spark.

"I hope your day was good to you," she said in the same husky voice she had used the night before when she had been taking about sex. "You must be working late or out partying. I hope you don't think I'm too forward I didn't think about much of anything but you today. I really want to talk to you again and I'll be home all evening. I may try to play some poker on-line, but you can call me anytime. Oh, and by the way, I got brave and took another picture of me that I'll send by e-mail after I hang up. You might want to check it out before you call me. I hope you like it. Damn! Maybe after you see it, you won't want to call me. Well, okay, bye for now."

His curiosity piqued as he snuffed out the cigarette and went to his computer. Waiting for Vivian's picture to arrive, Paul sorted through his inbox, which was cluttered with the usual Spam that had worked its way through his filtering program. All the time wondering what kind of picture Vivian would send him. Nude? All of her lovely breasts?

And then it arrived, titled: "Picture – Red Head?" There was also, an entry from Maureen and its subject "Reno/Tahoe." Shit, thought Paul. When it rains, it pours! All he had really wanted to do was to concentrate on Vivian.

Girding himself for his conflict, he opened Maureen's e-mail first.

> *Hi Paul. Sorry I wasn't at work today. My mother had some minor surgery (She's fine) and I needed to run her back and forth to the hospital.*
>
> *Have you given any thought to the weekends I suggested? I need to schedule it soon. I was only kidding about staking me to gambling money. I have some spare money and we should get separate rooms. Like you, I don't want anybody in the company to know about this, so it will be our little secret, even though nothing will happen. Right?*
>
> *Let me know. I'll be in the office tomorrow.*
>
> *M*

Well hell, thought Paul, what am I going to do with her? Maureen was certainly a good friend and he couldn't deny he thought of her often in ways that involved certain intimacies. Although Vivian sounded as though she could provide him with all the excitement that he needed and perhaps other things as well, Maureen was a known factor, the bird in hand, so to speak.

> *Maureen:*
>
> *Sorry to hear about your mother and glad she's fine. Guess she'll be well enough to watch the kids in a week or so? Let's plan on going to Tahoe weekend after next, which means in about 12 days. OK? I'll make room reservations for us at Harrah's for Saturday night. We can take off early Saturday morning and return leisurely Sunday afternoon..*
>
> *You're right, nothing should "happen," and this will definitely be on the "QT."*
>
> *Can you drive here to leave your car, as it will save us an hour if I do not have to drive to Sacramento to pick you up?*
>
> *See 'ya in the morning.*
>
> *P.*

Paul reviewed the message several times, finally deleting, and reentered the "nothing will happen" comment and finally changing "will" from "should." While he was on-line, he hit Harrah's Web Site and signed up for a Hold'em tournament being held that weekend as well as booking their rooms, non-smoking for Maureen and smoking for him.

Next, he opened Vivian's e-mail.

> *Paul I hope you got my voice mail message. I thought about you all day. I printed out that teasing picture of you in your robe and placed on my nightstand last night after we hung up. I got very brave this evening and took another picture of me, the one that's attached. I love my digital camera. I hope you like my picture. I could stand to lose about 5 to 10 pounds. This is in trade for a picture I'd like you to send me…. <blushing> with your robe completely open or no robe at all! You are an exciting man.*
>
> *Perhaps we can talk later; I'll be up for another hour or so. I'm not playing poker tonight.*
>
> *XO*
>
> *V.*

Checking on the attached picture, *Red Head?*, Paul was awestruck by what he saw on his nineteen inch, LCD monitor. Vivian was lying on her side, on a bed, completely naked. Her head was propped up on one arm and she was staring into the camera with a great sexy smile, her red hair cascading about her, her. Her breasts, although heavy, still had that firmness of those of a younger woman. Her legs extended almost to end of the bed, feet crossed at the ankles one of which sported a tattoo bracelet. The rise of her hip emphasized the curves of her body. Her neatly trimmed pubic hair was a dark brown which explained the question mark after the pictures title and a small butterfly tattoo was evident just to the side of it.

Instantly, Paul's penis, which had been at rest, started to come alive. Wow! She was something all right. Thinking that he could play that game, too, he left the computer to get out his camera. Rather than take a picture standing up, he decided to duplicate Vivian's image and placed the camera on its tripod next to his bed. After checking the focus and flash settings, he set the timer and lay down, mimicking her pose, his head propped on one hand, feet crossed at the ankles. He pulled on his cock just before the shutter went off to give him some additional flaccid length.

Transferring the image to his computer, he attached it to an e-mail.

> *Oh Vivian, you are a gorgeous sexy woman. Thank you so much for the picture. I just love it. Please don't lose any weight. You're perfect the way you are.*
>
> *I see why you named the picture what you did. You look delicious.*
>
> *I just took a picture of myself – at your request - <grin> and have attached one. I want you to notice, that, if you print out both of our pictures and hold them facing each other we can appear to be laying on the same bed, facing each other. I'll keep that thought and pray Vegas will arrive soon!*
>
> *I'll give you a call at 10:00 your time.*
>
> *XOXO*
>
> *P.*

After another much-needed cigarette and giving her time to receive what he had sent, Paul punched in Vivian's number. Apparently, she had caller ID because she didn't even bother to great him.

"I just love your picture." Her voice rose in pitch to a range that Paul was not used to hearing from her. Clearly, she was genuinely excited. "My, you are a big man!" She went on. "Yum! I'll place our pictures face-to-face as you suggested, but cannot wait to go skin-to-skin, as you put it."

Paul replied in kind, reminding himself how lucky he was at finding her, before going on to outline the timeline and tournament highlights. "Only forty-four days to go," he told her. "The tournament starts May 1 and ends on Cinco de Mayo, May 5. It should be quite a party! Let's review our travel plans. If I head out the evening of April 29 and drive about four hours and stay overnight somewhere, I can arrive after noon on April 30."

"Oh Paul I can't wait that long to see you!" she said and now her voice was that sexy contralto again. "I wish I could get some time off to fly and see you right now! Maybe I could figure out how I could get there for a weekend soon. What do you think?"

The blood started to drain from Paul's head. If he let her go off in that direction, it might mess up his weekend plans with Maureen and the trouble was he wanted his cake and eat it too. Playing poker well in the tournament was also paramount, and he needed to practice. Besides, he wanted to savor the meeting with Vivian in advance. And he wanted it to happen in Vegas where they could combine sex with high rolling poker.

"I'm looking at my calendar," Paul said, "Just what I was afraid of, every weekend has something. I have three weekends pretty well screwed up with an eNovalon client coming in on a Saturday. Then the following two Saturdays our president has two off-site meetings in a row, to do financial and strategic planning. I can't possibly get out of either one. So that puts us almost to the tournament."

"Well, it that's the way it has to be, that's it." Vivian said petulantly. "I just got so excited about seeing you sooner, but as we're going to be in Vegas for almost an entire week shortly after that I suppose I should save the airfare." Then as if it were an afterthought, "Why wouldn't this weekend work?"

"You'd have to fly tomorrow night," he reminded her, "and last minute airfares will be a killer. Besides, I have to get some important work done and if I don't it might jeopardize me going to Vegas. I promised my staff I'd come in this weekend."

"Well shit!" The word took Paul by surprise. "Speaking of airfare, I get in at 3:30 PM, on April 30. I'm flying Northwest out of Chicago." Do you think you could pick me up at the airport if you arrive in Vegas in time?"

Careful, thought Paul. He didn't really want to accede to her demands, if that was what it was, to early in this unknown relationship.

"Let's not plan on an airport pick-up right now," Paul told her. "Too many things can go wrong, traffic, flight delays, etcetera. If you have a cell phone, we could figure it out when you land. I've heard that The Four Queens has a terrific restaurant called Hugo's Cellar. If I get to the hotel before you, I can unpack and then meet you for dinner. You'll probably need to relax and have a cocktail anyway. Right?"

"I suppose you're right," she agreed, "but I'd love to just go to our room and make love before anything. I am so ready for you! Anyway, for the time being, we need to help each other pass the time quickly," she continued. "Lots of time to chat, trade more pictures, practice poker, and work on our plot."

"What plot is that?" Paul, asked, hoping she wasn't referring to his 'plan a robbery' comment. Paul had to remind himself that he had contacted Vivian first and not the other way around. She wasn't coming on to him on-line just because he was an expert poker player, expecting him to go along with some sort of plot, was she? Was she someone's shill, a front man? Or woman. The only thing that Paul was absolutely sure of, it was that she was all woman.

"Well I had some time at work today," she said, all business now. "And I did some research on the other players that will be playing in Vegas. I couldn't find an Internet reference for some of them, but there's a lot of information on-line about some of the better-known players like, Jamey Li, Brett Hoelscher. For example, these two guys have won over $500k so far this year. I also found a *Las Vegas Review Journal* article about a couple of bozo's that tried to rob Greg Raymer after a tournament at the Bellagio by forcing their way into his room. Raymer fought them off and they fled down the hall. Security cameras caught all the action and arrested these two morons within two hours. But, listen to this. Raymer did have a large sum of cash in his room!"

"You aren't suggesting we rob a winner are you?" Paul exclaimed. She was certainly taking Paul down several fantasy paths at the same time. It troubled him more than he could have thought. She sounds so serious about this one.

"I'm just fooling around but what if a sexy red head was to become very friendly with a player that has entered the final table? He's apt to have at least $100k in cash or a lot more. In addition, let's say I figure out how to get some sort of drug and then go to his room to help him celebrate. Knock him out and take the cash."

Knock him out and take the cash! What in hell was she thinking about? Or was she just trying one on to give him a jolt? Perhaps he should just play along, show her he could take a joke and run with it. Paul was not sure whether to encourage this thinking or shoot it down in its infancy. Surely she's joking, he hoped, but it was fun thinking about it. He said, "Vivian. You're going to be playing in the tournament. They'll know who you are. Cameras will catch you going into his room. He reports the robbery and the cops will be at your door. Strike that, since we'll be sharing a room, *our* door, in five minutes."

"But Paul," Vivian protested, "the point is there's a lot of cash around. We ought to figure out something. Don't you agree?"

"I think it's a great deal of fun thinking about the possibilities," he told her. "There's so much we don't know about security systems, whether or not the players are escorted to their rooms, or maybe they have to place their cash in the hotel safe. The incident at the Bellagio may have changed they way winners have to deal with their winnings. We'd be better off if you found a married guy to go to bed with and blackmailed him for the money."

Paul was relieved when their conversation returned to the logistics of their travel to Vegas. He volunteered to bring his CD player, a deck of cards, in case they decided to play strip poker, some candles, and booze.

Their conversation finally turned intimate again and when Vivian finally said good night, her parting words were, "Oh Paul, I can't wait to taste you. I'm salivating at the thought. Yum. Yum."

"Vivian I can't wait to taste you either," Paul said, not wanting to be outdone. "And examine that little butterfly a little more closely. Good night and sexy dreams."

Damn, Paul thought she really was something. He liked her a lot! But this bit about really planning a robbery bothered him. Of course, he knew she wasn't serious. It was just that different things turned different people on and if danger did it for Vivian, who was he not to go along with a bit of *what if.* It wasn't as though either of them were serious about it.

For the next several days, things seemed to straighten themselves at work and Paul and Vivian talked every night. They were getting to know each other very well, but Vivian wouldn't let up about planning a robbery, always asked him if he had come up with anything yet? Paul pretended he was still working on it and lied about checking up on security and surveillance systems on the Internet, changing the subject to sex, poker, the stock market, or music when her probing wouldn't cease.

One evening however, Vivian dropped a bombshell during one of their nightly chats. "Paul, I have something to admit," she said. "One of my boyfriends in Chicago actually belonged to the Mafia. I didn't know it at first, but I figured it out shortly after our first few dates. He called it The Family Business. Of course, this was over a year ago. Things did not work out romantically with us, but I still get an occasional e-mail from him."

Oh my God, Paul thought. What was this woman doing with a gangster for a friend? He had known from the start she was a loose cannon, but this was going too far.

"Anyway," she went on. "I found out later that he had pulled off some major swindles and robberies. It was art from big houses as I remember. I just loved the fact he always had plenty of money. I often told him I wanted to participate in something, but he always told me no."

Vivian took a breath so deep that Paul could hear the air rush into her lungs.

"The point is Paul, and please don't be mad at me, I sent RJ an e-mail and told him we were going to Vegas and asked him what he knew about casino security."

My God, Paul thought, she sounded as if she was actually serious.

"I was hoping that my e-mail question would make him call me," She went on with a note of something that sounded suspiciously like triumph in her voice. "And it did."

"Oh, Vivian, I wish you hadn't," Paul said. "if this man really is…"

"Please wait," she interrupted him. She was the business-like Vivian now, the Vivian that made Paul nervous. Sure, she promised superior sex, but at what cost? Not that he intended to go along with any of her ideas. "RJ isn't a dummy. From what he told me, he has never been busted or spent a day in jail. Besides, he's well connected."

"Anyway," She was saying, "RJ called me on the phone and told me he would check on a few things and get back to me, but wouldn't use e-mail to respond. In fact, he told me how to erase everything I'd already written on the subject. I didn't give him your name, but I did tell him I had a willing partner to commit a crime as there was going to be oodles of cash lying around at a poker tournament."

Good God, this was getting out of hand. Him a willing partner? No way. Did she have any idea what she was getting herself into? He had two choices now. He could hang up and not take any more of her calls. Or he could try to talk her out of this.

"Erasing the e-mail on your PC doesn't mean that a mail server somewhere doesn't have it. I know about this stuff. What exactly did your original e-mail say?"

"RJ taught me a lot about things like this too." Vivian replied crisply. "My original e-mail only said I was going to Vegas and was worried that hotel security had cameras everywhere and that I was going to be with someone I didn't want the world to know about. I thought it would force him to call me and it did. He said he might have an idea and that he would be sending us something so we could communicate. That's all I know for now. Isn't it exciting?"

Paul now wished he had never said anything about a caper. He just wanted to fuck, play poker and enjoy the good life. This was getting dangerous and complicated.

"My God, Vivian," he said. "I thought you were just kidding. Look, I have a good savings account, a good paying job with lots of stock options. If eNovalon makes it, I'll have all the money I'll ever need. Let's not pursue this."

"Look Paul," Vivian told him, "if there's any real danger or the risk is too high, RJ won't do anything. It wouldn't hurt to see what he comes up with, would it? You told me this was exciting, and you thought about it often, and I agree. If you're really uncomfortable, we'll drop it, I promise."

Paul had to make up his mind in a hurry and he did. This woman was not only sexy. She was opening the door to something inside him that he hadn't even known existed before. And he couldn't let that go. But that meant that he had to protect herself against herself. She was making a big mistake. People did that. And the only thing that he could do right now was to pretend to go along with the idea until he could find a way to talk her out of it.

"Okay, I guess." Paul trying hard to sound upbeat, said, "So, what do you think will happen next? I've got that stupid company conference this weekend." Paul lied, thinking of Maureen.

"We have a few weeks to see what RJ comes up with," Vivian said.

That was it as far as Paul was concerned. He couldn't let her go on talking about it. The best thing he could do was to change the subject and hope that she picked up on the fact that this sort of thing wasn't really his bag.

"I was looking at your pictures again and you really are beautiful." He said, bent on distracting her. "Our dinner at Hugo's won't pass fast enough, because once I see you in person I may just have to take you right there in the restaurant!"

"Paul, I wonder if I could get under the table and open your fly and lick and suck you right there in the restaurant. I can't wait to see you at full attention. Jeez, I'm getting wet just thinking about you."

Her comment made Paul think that maybe he ought not to insist on having dinner first. No! He preferred to see and talk to his women for a while, before bedding them. However, in this case, maybe . . .

Later, Paul wondered what this RJ was like. Was he a "Dem Guys," Yoze Guys" full of salty language or a more modern well-educated mafia type. Given what he knew of Vivian this man was probably a gentlemen and well spoken. On the other hand, did he know anything about Vivian except that she was one sexy number who really knew how to play poker. He fell asleep that night full of jangled nerves and doubts.

CHAPTER 6

PAUL AND MAUREEN went to lunch and worked out the logistics of traveling to Tahoe just a day away now. Paul's admonition to Maureen about keeping their weekend plans a secret did not actually go over well.

"Why Paul?" she demanded, "We're two unattached adults. The company doesn't have a policy against fraternization or dating. In fact, you know Lynn and Roger in accounting have moved in together, don't you? I know I originally said I'd like our weekend to be on the QT, but you know what? It doesn't really matter. Nobody has said anything. Everybody knows we are good friends and work together a lot. Why are you being so paranoid?"

Paul's initial explanation was not very articulate. He finally had to admit that keeping their trip quiet had a lot to do with the dicey situation he had put himself in when he had been caught fooling around with his secretary a few years ago, whereupon Maureen helped to convince him that their weekend was not the same thing. They would have separate rooms and neither of them were married. Therefore, she insisted, he should stop worrying about it.

When Paul reminded Maureen that he was taking this trip to Tahoe to help him tune up for the big game in Vegas next month, Maureen told him that she was not ready to play real poker and would be happy either watching him, if that was allowed, or, just playing video poker and slots. As for Vivian, he told her that the company meeting was going to be in a hotel in Sacramento and that he would hope he could find time to call from his cell phone Saturday night. Persistent as usual, she made him promise he would call.

On the day, Paul chose to wear a blue blazer, white golf shirt, and Levis. Having packed his small overnight bag, he slipped his bare feet into Sperry loafers, retrieved $5000 in cash from his book safe, which ought to be enough, particularly if he gave some to Maureen. He counted the balance at $14,500 and placed the book back on the shelf, making a mental note to withdraw some more cash from the bank if he did not win this weekend, so that he would have plenty in Vegas. Placing the money in his overnight bag, he secured the lock and reminded himself not let it out of his sight.

When Maureen arrived, Paul took in how she looked with appreciation. Dressed as she was in tight jeans and white tee shirt, her short, blond highlighted brown hair a mass of curls, she looked all of eighteen. Had she, Paul wondered hopefully chosen to dress so casually to encourage some fooling around? He had already decided that if the opportunity availed itself, he would have sex with Maureen in a nanosecond. The fact that being with her was simpler than with Vivian. He had known Maureen long enough to really like her and the thought of having sex with Maureen had always intrigued him. Vivian, maybe more sexy and desirous at a different level. Different level all right. Paul shuddered at his thoughts of crime and cheating.

During the obligatory tour of his eclectically furnished town house, Paul pointed out many of his prized possessions, including several Leroy Neiman paintings, including one of Stan Kenton, that was as he told Maureen, "his absolute favorite." When Maureen failed to recognize a sketch of the famous German composer Richard Wagner next to the Kenton, painting, Paul wondered if Vivian might catch the reason he placed Wagner and Kenton together on the same wall. Maureen marveled at his fifty-four inch plasma screen television, his Denon based stereo system with eight KEF speakers, and in the bedroom, his extra length king sized bed. The bed, surrounded by massive dark wood furniture, done in the style of the old world clearly overwhelmed the diminutive Maureen. While he tried to explain his computer set-up, Maureen, apparently distracted, ran her fingers across the varied titles of books on his library shelves, including leather bound issues of all the great classics, the complete works of Shakespeare, and his voluminous collection of poker and gambling volumes.

"I have a hunch I'm going to win in Tahoe this weekend." Maureen announced as Paul lit his last cigarette. Then, looking at Paul with the disgust non-smokers reserve for smokers, "Paul, aren't you afraid of the health consequences of smoking? Although I admit that it obviously didn't affect your growth."

Paul didn't respond to her smoking comment. He was used to them. And he decided not dash her hopes of winning with the "odds are really for the house speech." Instead, he asked how much money she had brought to gamble with. "I withdrew four hundred dollars from my mad-money account," she told him cheerfully. "That ought to be enough for the weekend, don't you think?"

"Oh sure it will," he replied, holding the door of the BMW open for her. "What you don't learn from that book you brought, I can teach you. Like how to play some keno and quarter slots. Four hundred dollars ought to last you while I play some poker. By the way, what kind of music do you like? I have several varieties loaded into the CD changer.

"I'm not fussy," Maureen said as he locked the door behind them. "I love all kinds of music. I know you like jazz and whatever you play will be fine."

There she was, saying things that made him think of Vivian. Vivian's musical tastes so matched his own, it was scary.

On the way to Tahoe, they listened to soft jazz and engaged in small talk about the scenery and possible weather in the Sierras. When Maureen picked up her book on *How to Win at Slots,* they lapsed into a silence that allowed Paul to remind himself of the trouble you can get in fooling around at work as he recalled the escapade with Sammie back in Southern California that could have cost him his career.

Ten years ago and soon after the now ex- Mrs. Helen Langley had turned frigid on him that he had become enamored with his secretary, Sammie, an intelligent, hard working lady in her mid-twenties with full breasts and shapely legs and naturally red, short curly hair. Marrying too young and having two children right away would have devastated a lesser woman, but Sammie was intelligent beyond her years, and knew enough to rid herself of a husband who was one of the "boys," always off hunting and drinking.

Sammie teased Paul all the time, leaning over his desk in order to display her impressively ample cleavage and it hadn't taken him long to start playing "sexy speak" games which ultimately led to making actual passes during their one-martini lunches. It was also clear that Sammie knew about Paul's eye for the ladies and suspected him of having an affair with one of the young women in the Xerox center downstairs although that was not true. Because of their frequent and candid conversations at lunch, she knew about Paul's marital problems.

Deep in thought, Paul almost forgot that Maureen was sitting next to him. He remembered as though it was yesterday, the night he and Sammie had worked late on some sort of budgeting project that was due on the president's desk first thing in the morning.

"How about I take you to dinner as a way of paying for your time here tonight?" Paul had asked.

Sammie's response had taken him by surprise. "How about we order in a pizza or something and eat right here? It's quiet. Nobody's around. We wouldn't be disturbed and I still have to tidy up a few files."

"Sounds great," he told her, "I can put on some music. I even have a bottle of wine stashed in my desk. We could have a little party."

"I'd love to party with you, here alone," she assured him. "Let me call the Pizza delivery. What do you want?"

Paul's answer surprised even himself, "What I want, is you!" And then added quickly, "Sammie, I'm sorry. I was being flippant. Better order the pizza. I like anything."

"Well, Paul, if you like anything, you can have me too." And with that, Sammie had moved very close to him.

Grabbing her around the waist, Paul had kissed her, hard and deep, delighted when she didn't recoil. Instead, she returned his kiss passionately, deeply, and boldly pressing her soft hips into his pelvis. Paul's experience over the years made him a good judge of what was going to happen and how fast, based on how his women initially returned his kiss. Damn, he thought, this was going to be fun.

He soon found out, however, just how aggressive Sammie could be. Despite Paul's admonitions about being caught in the office, she locked the door and turned off the bright florescent lights. Within minutes, Sammie was kneeling in front of him devouring his ample size alternately massaging his shaft with her wet, hot mouth, commenting on its size.

Soon, their clothes tossed helter skelter; he was kneeling on the floor between Sammie's spread legs. Paul had not made love to a natural redhead before and smiled when Sammie's red triangle enticed him to explore it. She had not wanted to let go of Paul's enormous, rock hard penis, and he had hard time moving away from her hand to provide pleasure to her sweet, red-carpeted spot with his lips and tongue, as her groans of pleasure echoed in his head.

"Oh God, Paul," Sammie muttered, between clenched teeth. "Please put that big thing in me. I want you now! I've fantasized about this for months!"

Not wasting any time, Sammie reached down and guided the head just inside her wet opening as she urged him to go slowly since she had never had a man so big. The carpet floor gave Sammie all the support she needed as he inched his thickness slowly into her hot, tight place. Her breasts received attention from his mouth as she continued to guide him into her.

"Oh God! That's' so wonderful." He still remembered the ecstasy in her voice.

He had moved in, slowly, slowly until finally he was all the way in, pinning her to the floor. He thrust slowly a few times, pulling out almost all the way and then inching his way back into her.

"I want you be still for a moment and feel the warmth and closeness of this moment," He had said as he lifted his weight off her, resting on his elbows. "Don't move."

As much as he longed to start thrusting in and out of her, Paul had controlled him-self. Sammie's legs and arms wrapped around him tightly when suddenly the door opened!

The little Hispanic janitor, pushing one of those big trashcans on wheels in front of her, let out a gasp as she saw Paul and Sammie entwined on the floor.

Sammie was clearly on the verge of having an orgasm when she and Paul both realized they were not alone, and froze.

"Shit! Paul exhaled, grabbing Sammie's discarded dress to cover her as the wide-eyed janitor backed out of his office and closed the door.

After they had dressed and Paul was straightening his desk, he said to Sammie, "Let's not get a pizza. I'll take you out. But I need to call Helen first."

Dinner was a somber affair as they thought of the dire consequences if the janitor told her superiors what she had seen. Paul's call home to tell Helen that he was going to be later that he had originally claimed hadn't gone over well, either. That was the night when Paul knew it was just a matter of time before Helen would ask for a divorce. Other than the financial consequences, it did not make him unhappy.

As for Sammie, Paul knew that he should break off the affair, but Sammie kept bringing them back on track with such suggestions as, "Let's play hooky tomorrow," or "Come over to my place soon."

Sammie confessed that her first husband, and an early teen lover, had both been small. Of course, she didn't know the difference about men and their different sizes until her best friend Mandy could not stop talking about her newest boyfriend. "God, so and so is so big!" Mandy would brag to Sammie. "If I were still married to my little Jeff, he could tell the difference if he had me again. I've stretched!"

Sammie told Paul she knew he was a big man just by looking at the bulge in the front of his pants. He told Sammie, "Hey, I'm not that huge," he told her, flushing, and "I've seen men with much bigger cocks. I'm just above average."

"No," Sammie protested, "You have to be way, way above average. I want to measure him very soon and prove it to you. I also need to brag to Mandy about what I've had."

In actuality, Paul thought, he hadn't seen larger men at all, at least in person. He was always thrilled when women told him this.

"Even though my marriage may be on the rocks, I'm still a respected senior executive and can't afford anything like this," he told her, not really reassured when she promised not to give his name.

Following that fateful evening, with Sammie, ten years ago, Paul had made himself a promise. If he escaped the situation without damaging his career, he would take an oath, not to fool around with any women at work ever again. He hated the feeling of being confronted with human resource types and particularly his boss, Ben Silver, who would have been so disappointed in him.

The problem was how to tell Sammie?

The next day he had walked by Sammie's desk on his way to his office, frowning that she was wearing a revealing dress that buttoned to just below her cleavage.

"Did you hear anything about last night?" he had asked her when she followed him inside and closed the door.

"Oh Paul," she cried, rushing into his arms. "I'm so sorry we almost got caught last night."

"What do you mean almost?" he demanded.

"I checked with Stan the maintenance manager, and simply asked him to check the logs because my desk seemed to have been disturbed. I said nothing was missing, but would he mind checking to see if the janitor had reported anything out of the ordinary happening last night. He just called back with nothing to report."

Breathing a little easier, Paul had returned her embrace.

"Sammie," he had said, beginning the speech he had been rehearsing during his commute. "We can't do this. Our careers cannot handle a scandal like this. If the custodian had reported what she saw, or worse, approached us for some sort of payment to keep quiet, we would have been toast."

"That means just here in the office, right?" Sammie said. "I agree with you on that, but please don't deny me the pleasure of finishing what we started last night. I really need you. In the year I've been your secretary, I've grown to love you, and I know, just by the way you treat me and look at me, that you love me a little too."

"I mean we can't be alone together anywhere," Paul had told her firmly. "I'm currently married, to a jealous wife and you can't risk losing your job with those two kids to feed. It just isn't safe, anywhere."

Sammie turned rigid in his arms. "Paul, please don't say that," she begged. "I'll quit my job. I can get another easily enough. My seniority doesn't mean crap. Promise me we can make love for hours and hours sometime soon."

That was when he had had to tell her that there was no future in their relationship, at least not the sort of future she should risk her career for. But he wasn't thinking strictly about himself. Whenever he thought about her two children, he was certain that that was not the direction in which he wanted to go. When she had left his office without a word, he had buried his head in his hands and, for the first time, in his life, wished that sex didn't seem to lead him in so many directions at once, and worse, that no real intimacy seemed to come of it, not even with his wife. Paul had thought that sexual expertise and technique was all he needed for true intimacy with his women. True, he was a pleaser, but that connection, that bond, that friendship, was always missing.

It was not long after this, while Sammie was still working for him, that Paul was given a huge promotion to run a plant for an aircraft parts manufacturer in Rockford, Illinois, far from Southern California, far from Sammie and far, as it turned out, from Helen too. After he settled into Rockford, he had filed for divorce, a divorce Helen had not contested. Assuming their debts, he fled with only one regret, that he had never really made it with Sammie. Now, as he turned the BMW through a series of long graceful curves, the snow-capped Sierras came into view and Maureen began to ooh and aah at the view, Paul told himself that he must be absolutely certain that there was never another Sammie in his life, unless, that is, such a relationship brought with it the romance, intimacy and unconditional love in both directions. Does it exist?

CHAPTER 7

"IT SAYS HERE that it's all a matter of money management," Maureen said, as they pushed their way into the Sierras. "Eighty percent of gamblers get ahead during a session, but eighty percent of those put it all back. Well, if I get ahead I'm going to keep it."

"That's right," Paul told her, relieved to be back in the present, "particularly playing regular slots and other table games. I'll show you how to play Keno. You might not ever get ahead, but if you get a big one it makes the losses bearable."

"Keno?"

"It's like bingo, only better because you play as an individual. It will be easy to show you when we get there."

As Paul continued to explain the merits and strategies of playing Keno, he glanced at the clock. They had been driving for over an hour, and he could use a smoke. What was it about gambling? He normally smoked only a few cigarettes a day, except when he was going to a casino, in a casino or leaving a casino. Then he put away almost a pack in an eight-hour period.

"Well, I could stretch my legs and hit the restroom," Maureen said as they approached an off-ramp. "Looks like you could use a stretch yourself, with your legs all bent like that." She touched his thigh, and Paul felt a spark of electricity dart between them.

After their short break, Paul accelerated the BMW smoothly up the onramp as they hurried on to Tahoe. Maureen was the first to speak as Paul sipped on his fresh coffee. "So Paul," she said, "tell me more about you and your secretary, the one that put you off office romances. What was her name, Sammie?"

Why in God's name had she brought that up now? Paul asked himself. But, since she had, he'd have to tell her something about, he supposed. But not all the vivid details.

"Yes, her name was Sammie" he said patiently, "and I really told you all there is. We almost got caught fooling around in my office."

"Yes you said that, but was it during the day? How far had you gone? What do you mean *almost* got caught? If you weren't caught, what happened? It's kind of exciting, imagining you being non-professional for once." Clearly, Maureen was not going to let up.

Paul's voice rose a bit. "Non-professional. What do you mean being non-professional? I have my moments."

"Well, at eNovalon, you're one of the older executives." Maureen explained, "I don't mean older like that's wrong. I think you're the perfect age. You're always so well dressed and you have great manners. You rarely swear and you handle crises like you've done it all your life. It is just exciting to see a chink in that professional veneer. So what happened?"

Paul sipped his coffee, and wondered how much to tell her, particularly since he had just remembered in detail the scenario with Sammie. He would never forget it.

Almost automatically, Paul started with his usual admonition, "Please don't tell anyone about this."

"I thought you knew me better than that," Maureen said, indignantly. "I would never repeat what you and I talk about, ever. Go ahead, I'm listening."

Paul started his story and left out many of the fine points that still aroused him when he thought about it. He finished with the janitor barging in the door.

"Oh my God!" Maureen interrupted, "Were you both naked?"

"Yes and needless to say it scared the "be-jesus" out of me, well, us. I was so concerned about it being reported. Hell, I had even opened a bottle of wine, which was against company regulations. I could have lost my job and my divorce would have been costlier that it was anyway. Turned out the poor little janitor was probably too embarrassed to report it. I was lucky. It could have been another executive walking in or a janitor with blackmail on his or her mind. I decided then, that fooling around at work or with someone from work just wasn't worth it."

As the words 'just wasn't worth it' tumbled out of him, Paul thought he might have gone too far, telling Maureen the story. Somehow, he felt better about telling her, but he didn't want her feeling that she fell into the same category as Sammie. He hoped it didn't ruin his chance with her.

"So, Maureen," he said. "I've been honest. Now let's hear about a chink in your professional armor. It's only fair you know."

"Okay," Maureen said, "but I have one question first. Make that a comment. I understand about screwing around at work, but I'm not sure that seeing somebody from work is still a valid concern in today's world."

Thank you Maureen, Paul thought. He really liked the way she was approaching this.

"I guess I have a couple of things in my past, I would have preferred hadn't happened. Remember Lou Staples in marketing? Well, he and I carried on for a few months early last year. I guess I was vulnerable to a man's attention just after my divorce. I was so unhappy in my marriage that it didn't take much for me to agree to go to dinner with Lou, and one thing led to another. I know he's not that attractive and he's still married, but we had a lot in common, including our failed and unhappy marriages."

Maureen's vulnerability had not shown at work. Paul was pleased and disappointed at the same time that she had been discreet, but had not shared what was going on with Lou with him. Maureen and he were close friends, but he guessed even the most private things are not often shared.

"So, my confession is that I had an affair with a married man," she went on. "A man from work, I might add although we didn't make love at work. He would come over to my house after the kids went to sleep. I felt so cheap after a few months of this. I finally told Lou that there wasn't a future in it for me. He took it hard as you might imagine. In fact, that's why he left eNovalon late last year and moved to Silicon Valley. I hear from him occasionally. He's still married and still in the software business."

It spoke well for Maureen, he supposed, that she actually cared about the fact that Lou's future hadn't been jeopardized. Paul had been listening intently wanting to ask more of the details about sex with Lou. He just could not imagine the attractive Maureen and Lou, awkward and unattractive as he was, struggling together.

"How about some other details about your sex life?" Paul said, with a newfound boldness.

"Well Paul, I hardly know what to say," Maureen said stiffly. "I've always found sex to be a very private thing. I'm uncomfortable sharing some details. Actually, I'd rather have sex than talk about it. But I guess I could tell you I lost my virginity after the senior prom in high school. It was not very good as a first experience goes. What about you?"

Paul told Maureen about his bout with the girl in his neighborhood when he was sixteen. He was trying to steer the conversation back to her when she startled him with; "Paul, I know we're having separate rooms and all and you said nothing should happen, but I'd like to know, I guess for my ego's sake, that you at least thought a little about us making love. Have you?"

Paul gulped silently and decided to be honest. "Yes Maureen I have thought about you, a lot. You know about my unwillingness to get involved with someone at work, but, yes, I have indeed fantasized about us making love. Has the thought occurred to you?"

"Paul, you're the catch of the office," she said, swiveling in the leather bucket seat to look at him. "I've thought about you in very intimate ways. I think my experience with Lou soured me on men for a while, but you always come to mind when I think about putting a man back in my life. But, I have to be careful though, because of my children. And then, of course their father is still around."

"Why does an ex being around make a difference?" Paul asked.

"He's very protective of them. When they visit they're always being pumped for information on me and if I'm dating and so forth. If he thought that I was having a man overnight, or he didn't think a new man in my life was right for them, he'd just be difficult to deal with. I don't want to put my kids through any more arguments or hassles. They had enough through the divorce."

Paul liked children, but the thought of being a step-dad to kids less than ten years old had always kept him from taking relationships with women with small children to the next level. After all, he had his retirement and full time poker playing to consider.

"The catch in the office, huh?" he said trying not to sound too pleased. "I suppose that, as the oldest man in the company, I do represent stability. However, actually I'm not that good a catch. I have some baggage and you already heard about some of it."

"Men will be men, I guess," Maureen said. "Sex is a great deal of fun, but I'm looking for a man who I can count on to be faithful, someone I can count on to help me raise Randy and Chelsea. I know that you're older and probably don't want to start a family at this stage in your life." Then as if another thought entered her mind. "What other baggage, Paul?"

Paul looked at the clock and odometer and figured that it would be nearly another hour for them to reach Harrah's. Pine trees filled the landscape as they climbed higher and higher. There was enough time to get it all out on the table. He'd better be careful though, she had set the bar high on what she was looking for in a man. The man for Maureen, that he was now sure, he couldn't meet her standards. Faithful and father didn't seem to describe him at all. With her honesty at what she was looking for, Paul now wondered if the weekend was going to be a bust as far as sex was concerned.

"I have a very wandering eye," he said. "During my two marriages and several longer-term live-ins, I was never faithful. I love women and I love pleasing them and making love to them. I also like talking to them, particularly to smart, vivacious, sexy women like you. What man wouldn't be tempted by you?"

That went pretty well, thought Paul. Never being faithful almost told all of it, didn't it? Then he added, "I guess I'm searching for the right one, but have a bad habit of wandering, or looking, while in a committed relationship."

"I think you're a heartbreaker, Paul," Maureen said. "I do believe you know how to treat women in bed and you're certainly a good listener. But most women want a commitment and honesty, not just good sex."

She seemed to be on to him, Paul thought, but he wanted to keep this subject on sex, which was what he really wanted. Didn't he? Yes. Maureen's figure, the shape of her hand, her curly hair, sexy smile. Yes, he wanted to bed her, but without hurting her. There was some sage advice he read sometime ago about never playing with a woman's heart.

"Great sex can't be under estimated." Paul told her. "I agree that sex by itself can't hold a relationship together in the long term, but without a good physical relationship to start with, a continuing partnership will fail. Take my second wife, Helen. She was an affair that got out of hand during my first marriage. She loved sex and she loved variety, a perfect combination as far as I'm concerned. When I finally left Shasta, my first wife, Helen and I lived together for several years before getting married. I was faithful to her during that time, but after we were married for several years, she lost interest in sex. At the same time, I thought it was the idea of being married that she didn't like. But now I think what happened was that she had an affair of her own and found out that a relationship like ours, based only on sex, wasn't what she wanted in life. Our marriage ended shortly after I moved to Illinois."

As he went silent, perhaps waiting for a comment from Maureen, Paul thought about what he had just said. A relationship just based on sex. Wasn't that what he had always wanted? Certainly true, but over the last few years, he had discovered that emptiness in his life, that good sex hadn't filled. He brought up the image of Vivian and recalled their conversations. Vivian it seemed provided a promise of a fulfillment in his life that had been lacking. Paul also knew and he believed Vivian knew that there was a connection between them. He didn't want to call it love, but it probably was that, at least it was an affinity. A certain kind of affinity of wit and quick understanding. What ever it was in their phone calls, and e-mails, Paul couldn't deny it. Love?

But he sure did like sex.

"Of course it could have been a lot of other things too." Paul added. "She was a country western fan and I hated it. She hated jazz. I was an executive and she was blue collar. We had very spirited debates on the merits of free enterprise and she was full of union ideology. I'm pretty much an atheist and she became a born again Christian! In the end, even great sex couldn't overcome all those other differences."

"So you were only faithful to Helen only while you were living together?" Maureen asked.

Oh boy, she's not going to leave it be, Paul thought. He wished he could express himself in these matters more articulately.

"I can't explain it," Paul said. He did not feel like elaborating nor could he. "That's just the way it was."

"Well, like I said, we're two consenting adults," she said. "However, let us just see how the weekend works out. No pressure from either one of us. Okay?"

"You've got it," said Paul, relieved. When they fell into a companionable silence as the mileage to Tahoe diminished. This self-examination made him uncomfortable, because it kept highlighting the hole he felt in his life right now. The hole that to now had been partially filled with sex, pleasing his partners and strokes to his ego.

CHAPTER 8

WHEN THE VALET drove off with the BMW, Paul picked up their small bags and walked past the poker tournament signs to the check-in counter. As they waited in the short V.I.P. registration line, they could hear the cacophony of bells and chimes coming from the casino, a combination of sounds that had the effect of an "upper" for Paul. His pulse quickened and he could not wait to play poker and some Keno.

"I hope you like your room," he said smiling at Maureen who was holding his hand. "We're probably on different floors as they usually separate smoking from non-smoking."

"That's fine with me," Maureen assured him. "I don't plan on spending much time in my room anyway. Of course, if I run out of money, maybe I'll have to. Hopefully they have HBO."

"Hey, I brought along some money for you to play with if you run low," Paul told her. "Don't want you to be all alone in your room with nothing to do."

He was grinning madly. Her smile and eye contact was a promising message.

"Meet me in the coffee shop in, say twenty minutes?" Paul said as he got off the elevator.

"No, give me thirty minutes," she said. "I need freshen up and call my mom and kids."

Paul thought at least with Vivian there would be no such calls to make.

Paul had just finished depositing the bundle of cash he had brought in the room safe, and had started to unpack when the phone rang. "Oh Jeez, Paul," Maureen said. "This room is huge and what a view of the lake! It's actually a suite. You shouldn't have spent this kind of money!"

"Trust me on this Maureen," Paul told her. "I'm not paying a dime for our rooms or our meals. All of Harrah's rated players get everything comped, meaning complimentary. I'm glad you like your room. Mine's not nearly as big."

He paused, hoping for some response, ideally an invitation for him to join her, but instead she went on about talking to her Mom and the kids and how she'd meet in the coffee shop afterward. Clearly she was still in the see-how-it-goes stage. Well he could deal with that. Patience was one of his virtues. Besides, this would give him time to put in that call to Vivian.

"We'll eat over at Llewellyn's in Harvey's for dinner," he told her. "It has a great view of the lake. Harrah's owns Harvey's so it will still be complimentary. I should be through with the tournament by seven-thirty or so. I'll make reservations and see you in a bit."

Paul thought about calling Vivian on his cell phone. If he was lucky, Vivian would be out, and he could just leave her a voice mail message. His conscious won. Or was it lose? He dialed Vivian's number. Luck was with him. Her voice mail picked up.

Relieved, he told her that he was calling between back-to-back meetings and that they were going to do some teamwork this evening so it didn't look as though he could call again but that he'd try in the morning. It was odd that, when he finished, the relief was gone. Suddenly he wished that there had been no need to lie.

Their lunch was pleasant and Maureen had a glass of Chardonnay. He could not help but notice that Maureen had apparently removed her bra because now he could see the jiggle of her small perky breasts when she laughed. Because it was cool in the restaurant, her nipples were well defined. He wondered if that was a signal. If she was going to be that subtle, a single weekend might not be long enough for him to initiate any action. Certainly, she was keeping the conversation innocuous enough.

"I thought the meals were all paid for?" she asked him now.

"Tips aren't covered by comps," he told her, looking at his watch, "I have about a half hour before poker starts. We need to get you a player's card and then find you a four-card Keno machine. I'll try and teach you how to play and, hopefully win."

They found two empty Keno machines in a row of several, and sat down. "I told you I have some money," she protested when he pulled out his sizable money clip and inserted four hundred dollars into Maureen's machine. "You didn't need to do that."

"The first Keno session is on me," Paul told her. "Now listen up. Let's play a dollar a card. Total four dollars. First, pick out your favorite four numbers on card A.

Maureen marked seventeen, eighteen, nine, and ten.

"Good," he said. "Just out of curiosity, where did you get those?"

"Okay," Paul continued after she had explained it was her two kid's birthdays, hers, and her moms. Did she, he wondered ever stop thinking about her family? "Now go to card B and select three of the same numbers, plus two different ones. Maureen followed his explanations all the way to card D, which had seven numbers now marked.

"Now we have four Keno cards: Card A has four numbers; B has five numbers; three of the same as A; C has six numbers, four the same as B, and D has seven numbers, six the same as C. Here is the trick. Hitting four out of four will pay you $91, five out of five will pay $810, six out six will pay $1632, and seven out of seven will pay $7000."

"Oh, God," Maureen gasped, "do you think I could hit a seven out of seven?"

"That's possible." Paul assured her. "The approximate likelihood of hitting your numbers is, you'll hit four out of four about one in 326 times. Hitting five out of five will come up about one in fifteen-hundred times, six out of six about one in seventy-seven hundred games and seven out of seven in about forty-thousand games. The odds at playing Keno really favor the house, but I've found that with these combinations you can keep playing longer and the longer you play the better the odds. Therefore, you should hit a four out of four before you run out of the initial $400. That will help you keep playing. Understand?"

"Yes, I think so. What's the most you've ever won playing Keno?"

"I've hit seven out of seven many times, once with four dollars in. It paid twenty-eight thousand dollars. It was a real nice hit. I can't say I'm ahead playing Keno, but even with some big wins, although rare, they sure are nice."

"Oh my God," was all Maureen could muster. "I'd faint dead away with a win like that."

"Don't count on it," Paul warned her. "You'll be lucky to hit a five out five before you run out of the original four hundred dollars."

Paul reached to his money clip again and gave Maureen another $400.

"It's fine," he said when she demurred. "I brought lots of money. If you win big, you can repay me. "Okay, you know what to do; I've got to get over to the tournament. Good luck."

He kissed her on the cheek.

On his way to the poker room, he looked back at Maureen, their eyes met. A very good sign that this could be one terrific weekend.

After paying the tournament entry fee of $125, he drew his seat assignment from the drum and headed over to table nine, with his $5,000 in chips, waving at Karen, John, and David, the regulars, seated at other tables.

The play was divided into three, three-hour sessions, the last round starting at nine-thirty tonight. These sessions would be divided into rounds. Rounds would last twenty minutes before doubling the blinds. A quick tournament, thought Paul. Harrah's wants us back in the casino as soon as possible. The first five players would share prize money of $10,000. which made it a very minor tournament compared to the Four Queens. He and Maureen would have plenty of time for dinner between sessions two and three, if he was still in it.

Paul tried to erase the thoughts of Maureen, Vivian and the "caper" she had suggested. The important thing was he had to get himself ready for Vegas. He had, after all, made a commitment to himself to play flawlessly and this might be one of his final opportunities to tune-up. Only one player at their table was familiar to him and after first name introductions, the dealer started.

Right from the start, Paul held his own winning a few small pots. On his next hand, he received pocket aces. He slow played and only raised half of the big blind. The flop had an ace so he was sitting on a set. Paul pushed out $2000 and watched, incredulous as every player folded. This was not a good omen, he thought as he raked in the small pot. Sitting next to Paul was a black man in his thirties, who was chewing on a toothpick. He had taken a good-sized pot early on and seemed to have the chip lead. After he won another pot, Paul, congratulated him and asked his name. James Roberts introduced himself as he raked in his pot and interestingly knew Paul's name.

"Yes, how did you know?" Paul asked, surprised.

"Oh, I heard about you qualifying for the Four Queens tournament. I just missed the cut. Good luck next month."

The reference to the Vegas tournament rattled Paul. Vivian's suggestion about a "caper" must have been bothering him more than he realized. He brushed the thought away. He needed to concentrate. He had already picked up a few tells from a woman across from him wearing a LA Dodger baseball hat, and a man wearing a cowboy hat and dark shades was working on keeping very still. As the second round started, doubling the blinds, nobody had been eliminated.

In the second round, Paul, in early position was dealt pocket kings and raised the $600 big blind to $2000., thinking he would take it right here only to be disappointed as the rest of the table all called him. It was now a big pot. They all watched the flop, K, nine, ten. The LA Dodger woman who had provided the small blind, this time was not "telling," bets $1000. Cowboy tossed in a $5000 chip. The

African American sitting next to him, called, and now, like the rest of the players, had just few chips left. With the top set of 3 Ks, Paul decided to reraise and go all in, all the while furiously trying to think what cards remained. Somebody could be holding a J, or a J and Q, or even a Q and eight, making straights a definite possibility, leaving him with two outs and hoping for another K or a pair to give him a full house which would give him fourteen chances to pull out a four-of-a-kind, or the full house, to beat any straight or flush.

Dodger Hat woman folded. Cowboy called Paul's all-in and the other two players and James folded. Cowboy turned his pocket Q-J, the top straight and nodded at Paul's pocket Ks, clearly aware that unless another K fell, Paul was going to be gone. The turn and river were five and six! Paul was done after only forty-five minutes. Incredible. Picking up his water bottle, he put his granny glasses in his pocket, congratulated the players, and left the room.

Could he admit to Maureen he'd been drummed out of the tournament already? One thing was clear; he had to play a lot better than that in Vegas. Sitting down at the end of a row of slots, he lit a cigarette, and thought about what he had just done. "Stupid play Langley!" he scolded himself repeatedly. He needed a drink and one of the prettiest cocktail servers he had come to know came by hawking her beverage service.

"Hi Lisa," Paul said, admiring her cleavage as usual which meant standing to give him a better view.

"Well, hi stranger," she said. "I haven't seen you in weeks. Are you drinking scotch or gin?"

"I'll take a gin and tonic," he said, feeling better already. "I came to play in the slot tournament and believe it or not, I'm already out. How are you doing up in here in Gods' country? Still married?"

"Same old, same old and yes, still married. You'll be the first to know if I am not." She giggled, "What's' a good looking guy like you doing all alone here again?"

"Oh I'm not alone this time." Paul grinned at her. "I brought a lady from the office. She's playing some Keno, and I just sat down here, feeling sorry for myself."

"Sorry to hear that." Lisa said and grinned again. "I'll be right back with that drink."

Paul watched her sway off and took in the slot players and the sounds and sights of the casino. Just as he doused his cigarette, Lisa returned with his drink. Tipping her $5, he headed off to Maureen's Keno bank, thinking there he went again, flirting with a woman for just the sake of it.

Drink in hand, Paul turned into the aisle with the Keno machines, and saw Maureen standing next to her blinking machine, jumping up and down, her small breasts bouncing up and down enticingly, while the slot attendant placed one hundred dollar bills into her open hand. As Paul got closer, he could hear the attendant counting, "...fifteen hundred, sixteen hundred, seventeen hundred, eighteen hundred, and eighteen forty. Good luck and do it again."

Paul got there just in time to place a twenty into the attendants' hand as Maureen was tucking her winnings and W-2G into her purse.

"Oh Paul," she said. "Look at that! I just won over $1800!" She leaned back and pulled Paul down to kiss him full and hard. "Oh thank you! Thank you! Are you on break?" she asked him. "How are you doing? Why did you give that man money and what do I do with this IRS thing?"

"Let's sit." Paul put his drink down on the Keno machine next to Maureen and swiveled towards her. "I've already lost because something distracted me and I made a dumb play. You're doing great, I see, and just so you know, it's customary to tip the attendants after a hand pay like that. As for the IRS form, they have to provide W2G's to all players who win more than twelve-hundred bucks. A copy goes to the government. You'll have to claim the winnings on your tax return, but don't worry. You can also claim you lost that much, so it will be a wash."

Maureen was still talking rapidly, on an excitement high, "No I didn't know you tipped them. Thanks, I really owe you now. I still have the second four hundred you gave me and look." She pointed to the credits on her machine. "I still have $204 left of the original four hundred you put in. Let me give you your money back."

"No, keep it for now. We have a lot of time left," Paul told her firmly. "I know the books tell you to quit while you're ahead, but a winning streak is a winning streak. Say, looks like your glass is empty. What are you drinking?"

"God, I've had two glasses of wine already. They sure come around often."

"That's the idea," Paul explained, "They want you to loose your judgment and spend more money than you would if you had all your wits you. Too much to drink also impairs your ability to make decisions, particularly when playing games where you have to think a bit, like poker, blackjack and even video poker. The house always works the angles. The way I played back there in the poker room, you'd think I was dead drunk! Say, let's play your machine down. You may as well use those credits. I always figure once I put the money in the machine, I've spent it."

"I'm so excited," She said. "Winning is a lot of fun, almost as much fun as…"

"Yes it is," Paul interrupted her. "I'll get us some more drinks, and play the machine next to you," he told her. "It would be nice if we both hit. I need to do something positive and exciting today."

"Oh Paul you'll be doing something positive and exciting today all right," Maureen said with a devilish grin. "I'll be right back. I need to go to the ladies room."

Paul watched her walk away, much as he did at the office. Only this time, thought Paul, he would soon find out how that cute butt looked naked!

"Looks like we have about three and half hours before dinner," Paul said when she returned. "If you're hungry before seven-thirty, I could move up our reservations."

"Oh no Paul. I'm still so excited. It will take me that long to be hungry for dinner. Are you going to play more poker?"

"Maybe after dinner, but for now I would just like to play some Keno with you. Let's see if we can't win again."

After Paul told her that the only time to change numbers was after a big win, Maureen selected a new series of four, five six and seven spots on her four cards and they played in relative silence for a while, getting several small hits, not running out of credits. The silence was only broken when Maureen thought of something else to buy with the money, mostly for her kids.

Paul yawned after finishing his third gin and tonic, and just as he hoped Maureen, motherly as usual, was quick to ask him if he was tired. Thinking fast, Paul told her that he missed his Saturday afternoon nap.

"We could go to my suite and relax a bit," Maureen said, her face lighting up. "Can we take our drinks with us?"

"That's a great idea," Paul told her. "Let's cash out. We can get the cash from our tickets later."

In Maureen's suite, Paul folded his blazer over the couch, kicked of his Sperry loafers, and placed his bare feet on the large glass coffee table. Sipping his drink, he gazed out at Lake Tahoe, which this time of day was a deep blue and shimmered in the sun thinking, not for the first time, that this was God's country.

"Sit down here and relax, Maureen," he said. "What a great view. The one from Llewellyn's is as spectacular and it's a bit closer to the lake. The sun will have set when we're there, but we should see a great twilight."

Kicking off her flats, she put her feet beside his on the coffee table. "Wow," she said. "look at the differences in the length of our legs."

"Yep, I'm a big'un all right and you're a cute one!" Paul said assuming a fake Texan accent. He placed his hand on Maureen's thigh and turned to her. Their eyes met and Maureen covered Paul's hand with hers. Paul felt that familiar stirring in his loins and could feel his desire starting. Not that his desire was ever far away.

"Do you want to get more comfortable?" Maureen said nervously. "Lie on the bed? I could turn on the TV and you could nap. I couldn't possibly doze off myself. I'm too wired! But you can if you like."

"Well, thanks," Paul said. "My back could do with a stretch out on the bed. You can turn on the TV if you want. You've already turned me on." Laughing, Paul uncoiled from the couch, and pulled her up with him, aware that he was being bold, but deciding what the hell. Pulling Maureen into him, he bent down, and kissed her hard, a kiss she returned passionately, wrapping her arms around his waist, while Paul stroked her bare back.

As Maureen pressed her small body into Paul's, his love member was growing quickly. When he cupped her breasts under her tee shirt, she gasped. "Please take me to bed!" she demanded.

When he lifted her off the table, she wrapped her legs around him and in two or three long strides, Paul was at the side of the bed and put her down. Stripping off the bedspread, he threw the dozens of pillows to the floor, and started to close the curtains.

"No way," Maureen panted. "I want to see you and I want to continue to see that incredible view."

Pulling off her tee shirt, Paul leaned down and kissed her nipples one at time, flicking his tongue as he pulled her small breast into his mouth. Maureen's hand moved to his fly and she began to rub his shaft through his Levi's and shorts.

Intent on slowing this whole thing down, Paul pulled her onto the bed, where she settled in, sitting astride him, leaning down to continue kissing him. His hands pushed against her breasts as she wiggled down and placed her crotch on his bulge. Finally, Paul reached down and undid her belt and button of her zip fly jeans. He slowly slid the zipper down as Maureen rose to give him access. Paul pulled off his golf shirt and Maureen slid her breasts onto his graying chest hair. Paul could feel her hard nipples pressing into him.

Reaching down he pushed her Levi's and panties down to her thighs, whereupon she pushed her pants all the way off, kicking them to the far corner of the room before undoing his belt and fly all the way. Naked now and clearly unashamed, she stood at the end of the bed and pulled off Paul's long Levis. Flinging them to the opposite side of the big room, she scrambled back on top of him and grabbed his erection.

"Oh God Paul, I knew you were big, but wow!"

Turning on one knee, she placed his penis in her mouth, guiding his thickness with two hands. Her tongue and lips were masterful: she seemed to devour every inch of him. Her moaning and sighing were an aphrodisiac as she licked and caressed him.

"Get up here." Paul finally commanded, whereupon she kissed him long and hard on the mouth. Hands on her naked buttocks, he pulled her up to his face and then as Maureen straddled his mouth, wiggled down so he could greet her opening, as she supported herself against the headboard. Paul's tongue tasted her oh, so, female wet area. Paul's hands covered her breasts as Maureen wiggled on his mouth. Her sighs and gasps of pleasure grew louder as Paul's experienced lips and tongue worked their magic.

After a few moments of what was obviously pure ecstasy, Maureen cried out, "I need you inside me now!" Grasping his cock, she slide down on his shaft. That initial feeling of insertion always overwhelmed Paul and he had to concentrate on not loosing control. Maureen's head bobbed up and down as, impaled, she lost herself.

For an instant, as Paul raised his head to watch, an image of Vivian flashed through his mind. For a split second, he thought he would just as well be happy with Maureen and not risk an association with the dangerous Vivian and her hoodlum ex-boyfriend. Maureen's scream of pleasure brought him back to the moment. Her orgasm was so intense that Paul could feel the convulsion of it.

Maureen collapsed on his chest. "Oh God Paul, that was wonderful!" she gasped. "But you you're still hard and big inside me."

"Let me finish on top of you." Paul, said, deftly moving their bodies in unison, until Maureen almost disappeared underneath him. Maureen wrapped her legs and arms around him and Paul started that thrusting he had learned so well. No two strokes were the same in intensity or length. All Maureen could do was to toss her head from side to side as Paul moved masterfully inside her. Soon he, too, had the intense experience of pleasure.

After Paul had rolled off her, they lay quietly beside each other, silent each knowing the other was content. The warm sun was streaming in the window they could see the far shore of Lake Tahoe and a sliver of water shimmering in the sun.

Paul soon dozed off into one of those peaceful after-sex naps. When he awoke, Maureen was sitting on the couch, looking out at the sunset. She had put on her tee shirt, folded Paul's clothes, and placed them neatly at the foot of the bed. Paul rubbed his eyes and glanced at the clock. He had been asleep for forty-five minutes. "Hi there sexy," Paul muttered.

"Good morning sunshine." Maureen joked, coming to sit down next to him. "Paul," she said, leaning over to kiss him. "That was great sex. It was wonderful."

"You're fantastic, too," Paul said and meant it. He was looking at Maureen in a new light now. Clearly, she was sexy as well as bright. Maureen would rank right up their near the top of his considerable list of women, whose sexiness and companionship never left his memory.

Dinner at Llewellyn's was very pleasant indeed. The food was outstanding, the service impeccable and the view breathtaking. Paul had ordered the Porterhouse, rare, while Maureen settled for the salmon. Against his better poker playing judgment, Paul ordered his favorite martini composed of Blue Bombay Safire gin, olives, twist and slightly dirty, up. Maureen stayed with her Chardonnay and couldn't 'possibly have any more to drink' after her second glass of wine. Paul ordered a nice Shiraz to go with his dinner. They talked a lot about work, her kids, and her ex-husband, who was really a jerk. Paul nodded and listened intently, as was his usual custom, when he was with bright, sexy women.

CHAPTER 9

BY THE TIME he and Maureen had kissed goodbye and she was on her way to her home in Sacramento, Paul was just plain relieved. She had spoken to her mom and kids from her cell phone in the car, broaching the subject of taking some time off for a vacation without the kids. Paul could tell from her side of the conversation that Maureen's mom was telling her that it was not a good idea right now. Apparently she was not sure she could watch the kids for that long. Perhaps, Paul thought, he wouldn't have to put the arm on Ted to deny Maureen time-off after all.

When he got home, a plain brown envelope with a post office box return address from Oakbrook, IL, was waiting for him in the mail. Paul opened the letter on his patio and found a carefully hand printed note, which read:

Paul,

Vivian has told me about you.

My cell phone number is below.

Call me when you receive this. We need to discuss when and where we will meet in Vegas.

RJ

Shit, thought Paul, Vivian must have given the man his address. The last thing he needed was some gangster type wheeling and dealing with his life. There was nothing meaningful in the cryptic note. All it did was raise the hair on the back of his head. In no mood to call RJ right now, he needed to think about all of this, although he should call Vivian first. Earlier he had noticed his message light blinking, and now it occurred to him that probably she had called him.

Voice mail announced one message, but his caller ID indicated three calls, all from Vivian Davis. "Hi you sexy man, whose body I can't wait to ravage," Vivian said in her best sultry accent. "I called a couple of times but I didn't leave a message until now. Then I tried to call your cell phone, figuring I could catch you on a break or driving home, but you must have turned it off or something. You'll need a vacation after working these weekends. eNovalon is lucky to have you. I hope you're okay. Please give me a call. I've missed you. Hugs and kisses." Just before Paul was about to hit the delete key, Vivian added. "Oh, by the way, remind me to tell you about my great winning streak on Casinoholdem last night."

Paul grinned. His scheme had worked. Vivian was convinced he was working and would not have a clue that he had spent the weekend with another woman.

Maureen!

What was he going to with her?

Paul busied himself with e-mails before calling Vivian, deciding he would call RJ next to tell him that despite what Vivian may have said to the contrary, he wasn't interested in setting out on a criminal career.

Vivian declared herself delighted to hear from him. It seemed that she had won over a $1000 in about four hours of play. Had he heard from RJ?

"I received a short note with his cell phone number," Paul said, refraining from rebuking her for having given RJ his address. 'He wants me to call him. You know, Vivian, I think it's time to put a stop to this right now.'

"I thought we agreed to just find out what he had in mind," Vivian reminded him.

So it wasn't going to be that easy to get her to forget the whole thing. He should have known it wouldn't, he supposed. Well, he wasn't going to let her go it alone. With that in mind, and only that, he promised to make the call.

Paul promised to call her after his initial chat with RJ.

As he punched in RJ's cell phone number, Paul realized he was sweating.

"This is Vivian's friend," he said when a man answered.

"She's told me a lot about you." The voice was low pitched and gruff. "No names on the phone. Is that clear?"

"Got it." Paul replied succinctly. Holy Mother, what had he gotten himself into? Well, actually, he hadn't done anything wrong yet. And he certainly didn't intend to. Paul flashed on a picture of himself sinking into murky water somewhere wearing cement shoes.

"Good," RJ continued, "Ok, here is what I have so far. I have some contacts in Vegas and with the hotel that is hosting the event. The hotel hasn't had an event like this before and is trying to cash in on the current craze for Texas Hold 'em, but we have a good idea of how this is going to work. They're going to re-configure a large meeting room to host the event, because they have no other space. Which means that they will have less observation and by that I mean primarily overhead security cameras."

If he hadn't been sure that he had to keep Vivian out of this before, Paul was certain now.

"I have layouts and schedules and my contacts believe we have come up with a very low risk plan to do what you and she discussed." RJ went on in a business-like voice. He certainly, didn't sound like a member of the cast of *The Sopranos*. "It will take perfect timing. I understand you and she plan on arriving the day before the tournament starts. We'll need to meet at a place other than the host site, probably late on the arrival date or first thing the next day. We'll have five full days to plan while you both participate in the tournament. That should give us time. I have one very important question for you. What are the chances of one or both of you making it to the finals?"

Paul took a deep breath at the question. He would have to play a lot better than this weekend to answer RJ's question affirmatively with any conviction. Or perhaps he should just ask why the fuck is that important? Torn with providing the answer or asking a ton of is own questions, Paul simply said, "We're both very good players, but I think the odds are only even that one or both of us make it to the finals. The other players are excellent and well seasoned in tournament play. Also, luck can be a deciding factor."

"It's important that one of you get to *that* table," RJ said firmly. "Vivian gave me your cell phone number. I'll call you again one evening next week with some other details."

Mulling over the conversation in his mind, Paul realized RJ was a very serious fellow and had to let that all sink in before he called Vivian. Did he dare think RJ was competent in all this? What was their role to be? Or rather Vivian's role. Paul already knew his, which was to play along until he was certain she was not implicated

He called Vivian after more contemplation about all this nonsense. To the question as to whether she would make it to the final table, Vivian's latest round of winning was reflected in her answer, that of course they'd make it. After their conversation, Paul thought to himself, hey, a few days ago I was feeling bored, unfulfilled, and the lack of excitement in his life quite apparent. Now he has a woman he really cares about. Cares enough to protect her from this insane involvement with some stupid hood.

The next morning, Paul was going through his e-mail list when Maureen knocked on his office door. "How was your weekend?" she said, giving him a wicked smile.

"Absolutely perfect," Paul told her straight faced. "I really got lucky."

"You went to Tahoe and got lucky playing poker?" Maureen said, loud enough so that everyone in the outer office could hear. "Well good for you! Listen," she added in a sotto voce. "I thought you'd like to know that my mom can't watch the kids in a couple of weeks, and you know I won't let anyone else sit with them overnight. So," she went on, leaning way over his desk, nervously fingering his paperclip holder, "we'll just have to go to Tahoe again next weekend."

It was amazing, Paul thought, how much women took on themselves once they thought that a relationship was established. He liked Maureen a lot and he knew he had made that clear. But there had never been a time when he had given her a clue that he was going to let her set his schedule for him. And then he reminded himself to be fair. Vivian was dashing. She offered excitement. And if he weren't careful, she might take him over the edge with her. But Maureen had no hidden agenda's. That ought to give him a good deal of pleasure. And perhaps, if he'd just let himself, it would. Vivian offered a world of excitement, some wonderful musical and intellectual compatibility, danger and God knows what else. Maureen, on the other hand, was a single parent of two, looking for a husband and/or father. Both women brought some plusses and minuses with them. He would have to walk these two tightropes more carefully than he usually did.

"Sorry Maureen," he lied. "I can't next weekend. A friend is driving over from San Francisco. We've planned it for a month or so. I couldn't get out of it."

Maureen looked hurt and disappointed. "You didn't mention you were tied up that weekend when we were looking at dates to go to Tahoe. What's *her* name?"

"*His* name is Fred," Paul told her, "and I forgot about it until I saw it on my calendar last night. Again, I am so sorry, Maureen. You know how much I'd love to go to Tahoe again. How about when I get back from Vegas? It's only a few weeks, and I really want to. You must know that."

"Well then, we need to work out some other time to be together very soon," Maureen said frowning. "My Mom is flexible. It's just that she can't watch the kids when you go to Vegas. Let's say we have dinner and, well, you know, after work one day this week. I can get to your house in forty-five minutes. Just let me know."

"You got it," Paul said, relieved enough to ask her to lunch.

As he watched her swing her cute ass in her professionally cut lavender suit as she walked down the hall from his office, Paul reprimanded himself for compounding all these lies. Now he has to keep them all straight. This was worse than when he was sneaking around when he had been married!

When Maureen and Paul were settled side-by-side into one of the back booths at the local steakhouse, they made sure there were no other eNovalon employees around before they kissed. "I just can wait to be close to you again," Maureen whispered. "Have you checked to see what night we can do dinner? My only problem this week is Thursday. Other than that, I'm very available."

It was a good thing, Paul thought, that he loved aggressive women and competent female business managers. Any more aggressive, Paul thought and Maureen would be borderline pushy. And speaking of pushy. What about Vivian simply assuming that he'd be willing to join her in a criminal enterprise.

"Why don't you come over to my house after work, on Wednesday?" Paul said. "I'll open a good bottle of wine and throw some steaks on the Bar-B-Que. How does that sound?"

"Sounds wonderful. I just can't wait." Maureen placed his hand on her thigh and spread her legs slightly. "I'll bring desert."

The rest of the afternoon passed uneventfully. Paul loaded several rough-draft sales brochures on eNovalon's implementation methodology into his briefcase as he tidied his office for departure, promising Maureen he'd review them tonight since they needed his final approval and mark-up before going to the printer tomorrow.

Driving home to the sounds of Henry Mancini, Paul mentally ticking off his schedule for the next week or so. It was going to be a busy one, involving as it did, Maureen, Vivian, RJ, work, and poker practice. He decided to use his visit from "Fred" to return to Tahoe for a couple more practice sessions. Without any distraction of the sort Maureen had provided, he would do better than last weekend. Additionally, since Vivian thought he was going to be attending his "company meeting" he would not be spending time on the phone to her with long, intimate chats. He wanted to show Vivian, and more likely RJ, he could play poker with the best of them. For whatever reason, RJ said one of them had to get to the final table. He hoped to hear more details very soon. Paul admitted to himself, that he was feeling very anxious about the whole thing, including satisfying what appeared to be the insatiable, Vivian.

Before Paul settled in at his kitchen table to eat his frozen dinner, consisting of some mystery meat and off-white rice, he remembered to charge and keep his cell phone with him. He looked at it sitting there on the table next to his plastic tray wondering what it might bring to his life. Excitement. Danger. Police problems. Mafia issues. He shuddered to think of all the consequences of plans gone wrong. He was anxious to hear from RJ so he could decide how he could best go about keeping Vivian from incriminating herself.

After checking his e-mail, Paul pulled out the printer's copy of the brochure he needed to proof and approve for Maureen. Just as he started to edit the copies, his cell phone rang.

Out of habit, Paul almost identified himself when he answered, but bit his tongue even though it could be a legitimate business call.

It was RJ's voice on the other end, not Vivian's as he had hoped.

"Okay," he said in a low voice, "Now listen carefully. I've talked to her but I didn't tell her as much as I'm going to tell you, because frankly I'm not sure she's a good listener."

That surprised Paul, as Vivian among other things, was, as far as he could tell, an excellent listener.

"The plan is taking shape," RJ went on. "We have some inside information from ESPN that is televising the event. I'll meet you in the parking lot of the local baseball park in Vegas at eleven the night you arrive. For reasons I'll explain then, I can't enter the host site although I understand you'll both be there for several hours before that. Expect one or more men to be accompanying me. Park in the most vacant spot directly behind home plate. She'll recognize me. The two of you will then follow me in the car to another spot where we'll be a lot freer to talk. I'll tell you where later. At that time, I'll provide you with some props you'll need to carry out the plan. This will all make sense when we meet in person. Are you okay with this?"

"Actually, no, I'm not," Paul said firmly. "I need to know a lot more and I want some assurances from you before I agree to meet."

"Such as?" RJ said, sounding annoyed. Apparently, he was not accustomed to people asking questions.

"Such as, what props? Who are these other guys? Right now, how risky is it for me to just talk to you? Can these conversations be tapped? I'd like some assurances about safety. Will there be guns? What are the props and why is it important to be at the final table?"

Paul's stream of questions were greeted by a low, guttural laugh. "Well, those are quite valid concerns," RJ said. "and now I like you more for actually asking them. You should be concerned about all those things. Let me just say this, it will all become quite clear when we meet, but for now you'll just have to trust me."

"I'm not sure I want to trust you without more information."

"Fair enough," RJ said, "But, *I'm trusting* you right now. I only have her word that you're okay, and not a cop or a person that would talk about this to anyone. This is dangerous shit, but you know what? It can be a mighty nice payday."

"So you're not going to answer my questions or address my concerns?"

"Not until we meet. That's just the way it will be. You'll still have time to back out, but I really believe when you hear the plan, you'll be ready and eager. And incidentally, I don't plan to use phones to communicate again. I've told her the same thing. You and she should use your normal means of communicating. However, don't discuss any of this."

And with that, he hung up. Damn, thought Paul. Lighting another cigarette, he went over the few details he was now in possession of. God, he hoped that one of the props wasn't a gun! And how does ESPN information fit in? There were just too many questions left unanswered. Still, as RJ had said he could back out anytime after listening to the plan. Tell RJ, nope, too risky and too soon. RJ could still take Vivian down this path to doom. That was the important thing, Paul remained himself, because if he didn't pretend to go along with this, Vivian was just enough of a loose cannon to go it alone. He concentrated on the positive aspects of the Vegas trip, Vivian and the tournament.

The baseball park, Cashman Field, according to Mapquest was less than ten minutes from the Four Queens. Paul assumed RJ would know the parking lot was safe from surveillance as well. If there was anything he didn't want, it was for him and Vivian to be picked up by the police in the presence of a member of the Mafia.

He had just finished marking up the brochures for Maureen when his regular phone rang. The caller ID displaying Vivian's name.

"Did you hear from him?" she asked before Paul had a chance to say hello.

"Yes, I did," he told her. "Just a little bit ago." "Not very satisfying in terms of answering questions, but I know the next time we officially communicate we will be there. I'm still very anxious about the whole thing, but I'll wait to pass judgment until then. And I want you to promise me this. If I don't think this is safe – well, foolproof actually – and decide to drop out, you won't go along with him. Can I count on that?"

"Paul, come on," Vivian pleaded. "RJ is smart and can be trusted to make this work. I promise.

Not exactly a promise to bail out if I decide to, thought Paul. This may be more difficult to manage than I thought.

"Please forgive this question," Paul said, opting to not press for an outright promise right now. "But I have to be sure about all this. Is there any reason, given your past relationship with that man that would make him want to get even with you? I realize we've been warned about talking about this on the phone, but right now I don't care and I need to know. For instance, is he using this caper to get you caught and put in jail, or worse, put you in danger where you could lose your life? Maybe he's angry with me, because I'm entering your life. And what does RJ stand for? What's his real name? Please tell me the truth. Our careers and lives could be resting on this."

Vivian sighed, "Oh Paul, not to worry. He and I really did depart on the best of terms. I'll tell you all about that and give you his full name when we meet. I really think speaking about him on the phone, like he said, should be avoided and remember, *it* was me that came up with this whole idea. Not him."

Paul started, "Yes, but what…"

"Please don't worry," Vivian interrupted him. "He really has no motive for us. He's in it for the money, just the way we're in it for the excitement *and* the money. Believe me, combining this caper with really great poker and terrific sex will blow your mind."

"Ok," Paul replied, "It's just that I've never done anything like this, and I want all the cards on the table. In my opinion, the risks are pretty high. At least send me his name via e-mail. That should be safe enough."

"I'll do that and I agree," said Vivian. "I've never done anything like it before either, although, like you, I've always wanted to."

After another half-hour of chatting about poker, politics and sex, Paul told her that he should log on to Casinoholdem to get some practice, particularly as he couldn't tomorrow night.

"I have another sales dinner," he lied. "Are you going to play tonight, too?"

"Not tonight," she said, assuming her sexiest voice, "I think I'll go to bed and dream about you. Oh and by the way, I'm going to send you an e-mail after we hang up. I'll send that name you asked for and I've made up a limerick about us. It's probably just dumb, but enjoy it anyway."

After hanging up, Paul checked his e-mails. One with the subject "Dinner," was from Maureen. He was about to open it when Vivian's e-mail arrived.

He opened Vivian's first:

Hi Paul. I think about you way too much at work. I had to snicker to myself 'cause I came up with this limerick:

"When Vivian started flirting with Paul.

She feared she might not take it all

She soon realized,

That because of his size,
"Oh mercy!" she surely would call"

Dumb, I know, but I keep thinking of your picture and how wonderful this is going to be.

Fondly thinking of you and will talk to you tonight.

Viv

PS. Rocco Justini.

The limerick made Paul smile. He responded:

Very cute Vivian, just like you. Not only are you cute, you are downright gorgeous and oh my gosh so darn sexy!!! I can't wait either.

I'll have to brush up on my limerick writing and come up with something to reciprocate.

Thanks for the name.

XO

P

Paul memorized the name at the bottom of Vivian's e-mail and deleted it. If he had a chance, he'd look it up on the Internet and see what he could find. Next, Paul opened Maureen's e-mail:

Hi handsome;

Just realized that we didn't agree on a time for me to come over on Wednesday. How about 6:45? I should be able to leave my house about 6:00. I'll bring a salad. I have a very busy day tomorrow and wanted to make sure we had a time set before Wednesday.

XO

Me.

Making a mental note that he needed to pick up some steaks and wine tomorrow on the way home from work Paul turned his mind to the Tahoe get away this weekend. After busying himself marking up the sales brochure for Maureen, he decided not to play poker tonight. He had a lot to think about and turned in early.

Wednesday evening came soon enough and Paul started the gas grill in anticipation of Maureen's arrival, after opening a very good bottle of Australian Shiraz to let it breathe. He checked his bedroom, threw some dirty clothes in his clothes hamper, pulled the bedspread taut, checked the thermostat, and returned to his patio for a cigarette. Maureen would arrive at any minute.

Maureen had changed from a suit into a floral short skirt and plain white blouse, her white flat pumps making her bare legs look even longer than they really were. Their greeting was intimate and passionate. Maureen pressed her body into his and excitedly moved her hands up and down Paul's back. For a moment, there was a distinct possibility that they might not get to dinner for quite a while. But they did and it was actually very pleasant. Maureen's salad was a wonderful mixture of lettuce, walnuts, diced vegetables, and dried cranberries, and they chased their perfectly cooked, medium rare steaks down with the excellent Shiraz.

"Thanks for dinner," Maureen said as she relaxed on the big leather couch. "Now about that desert." She kissed him on the lips, long and hard.

The lovemaking that followed was lustful and romantic and at the same time tender moments were followed by their overwhelming desires to meld into one. But Maureen had almost been too anxious, too aroused. Could she be acting or just desperate for his companionship and more?

After Maureen left around midnight, Paul started thinking about how he could ease her down. He really cared for her and obviously, she was, at least, in lust with him. However, with those two young kids and the age difference between her and him, it was hard to imagine their relationship going any further than this. Furthermore, they had to work together. And that was another problem, one that would ultimately complicate how the relationship would end. But the important thing was that the relationship had to come to end, at least temporarily because Vivian and Las Vegas loomed just over a week away. At nearly fifty his recovery time, although still good, was not like what it had been twenty years younger.

Deciding that he'd better do some research on this RJ character, Paul fired up his computer, entered Rocco Justini in the Google search engine, and waited. Only one hit from the *Chicago Sun Times* appeared. Disappointed that what he pulled up didn't include a picture, Paul read the article, and began to sweat. This guy could be dangerous.

> ***CHICAGO*** *-- A federal judge Friday dismissed extortion charges against alleged Mafia member Rocco Justini of Chicago, Illinois.*
>
> *Justini pleaded not guilty to racketeering and conspiracy charges, stemming from a police sting more than three years ago. The eight-day hearing followed two years of court motions on the admissibility of certain evidence. In light of the judge's ruling, prosecutors said they would review their options to pursue the arrest and conviction of Justini, known as "RJ" amongst his family and friends.*
>
> *The hearing regarding Raymond Castaldi, arrested at the same time as Justini will be continued next month. Federal prosecutors having been seeking arrest warrants for others caught in the sting operation.*
>
> *Justini's attorney, Martin Bayliff, speaking for the defendant, "Mr. Justini has never been a member of the Mafia and is very happy with the ruling and is looking forward to getting on with his life."*

Finding sleep hard to come by, Paul found his serious, deepest thoughts jumping from Maureen, to Vivian, the dangerous plot, the obviously treacherous RJ, and wondering what on earth life had in store for him over the next few weeks.

CHAPTER 10

PAUL WAS ABOUT an hour on the road to Tahoe listening to pulsing big band of Rob McConnell when he started thinking about last night's Casinoholdem play with Vivian. They had been on the phone for their nightly chat and decided to log on and play while still carrying on their conversation, both managing to maneuver to the same $10/$20 table.

While talking to each other on the phone, revealing each other's pocket cards paid-off handsomely several times, Paul constantly reminding himself that he would never have done this if it weren't for the hope that this would provide Vivian with just enough excitement so that she could forget RJ. One hand as specifically outstanding: Vivian had pocket K's and Paul's pocket contained two Q's. Upon the declaration they had half the Q's and K's between them, Paul suggested they alternately raise to the limit each betting round before the flop. The flop revealed a K and Q and a harmless six.

"Oh God, Paul," Vivian had shrilled, "We have the market on kings and queens. Too bad this is not no-limit. What should we do?"

"Let's be careful," he warned her, "Three players are still in and have called all of our raises. We're still in the power seats, but if one of them has pocket sixes and the turn or river has another six, we'll be toast unless one of us gets another king or queen. Let's see what happens. Keep raising and we'll call each other."

Incredibly, the turn had a K. "Oh Paul, we have 'em!" Vivian told him. "Let's keep going."

They tried to move the table before the river, but even at this level of low stakes, the other players folded. Vivian's winning balance, however, went up nicely.

After the game and a couple more "shared" pots, Vivian suggested that they use the strategy in Vegas if they were at the same table.

"Well, if we get to the same table in an early round, one of us will get knocked out of the tournament," Paul reminded her.

"But it might be worth making sure one of us moves on," Vivian said. "Particularly since *he* said one of us needs to get to the final. We should think about a way to communicate that won't get us caught."

After protesting that they didn't need to cheat, Paul promised Vivian he would give it some thought while he was attending the "company off-site meeting." Anything to distract her from becoming involved with RJ. Vivian's willingness to cheat, although didn't surprise him, given her penchant to participate in the plot, disappointed him. Was he even thinking about it, because she was so darn sexy?

Buying $500 in chips for the $20/40 table, Paul settled into his assigned seat, and nodded at the other players, none of whom he recognized this time. From the various sizes of chips stacked in front of them, most had been playing awhile. One of the older men players eyed him, with that "Ah, fresh meat" look.

Paul had played enough poker to have developed considerable skill at shuffling a stack of five chips into another stack of five with one hand, although he usually did not handle his chips unnecessarily because he had learned that it could give unwanted tells to other players. But this time he had decided to produce a pattern of chips that could communicate the cards he had in the pocket to Vivian when they reached the tournament in Vegas. If he were lucky, he might think of something fascinating enough to distract her from thinking about going along with RJ's hair-brained scheme.

After about an hour of play, during which Paul was ahead a few hundred dollars, he thought he had a good system of signals, which a knowledgeable player, overhead camera, or dealer might not catch, a pattern he would or wouldn't share with Vivian. He'd have to think on it. He had never imagined himself cheating at a game he loved as much as he did poker, but radical situations demanded radical solutions.

Since there were three denomination chips at most poker tables, but sometime only two he came up with a set of chips that could transmit each pocket card, without suits. They would only use the system for pairs and any 10, J, Q, K or A. Pairs less than ten would be just that. A pair less then ten would be a stack of five chips and then two high denomination chips placed, for just a moment, on top of the five chips. Then, during each hand, he would have to shuffle and separate the chips as if this was a nervous quirk.

For a pair of 10s, Js, Qs, Ks, and Aces he would place the two higher denomination chips on the bottom of the stack of five for a moment. Using two chips over and under would raise less suspicion. However, indicating the exact value of the card would take some thinking about.

Figuring that it was only important to know about the value of five cards the 10, J, Q, K, A, he developed a way to let five chips fall to the felt tabletop with his left hand in patterns of five. Holding the five chips, he practiced letting one chip fall, then placed the other four on the single chip. If he previously placed two higher denomination chips on the bottom of the stack of five, reshuffled the chips and picked up the stack of five and let one fall, quickly placing the remaining four on top, it meant he had a pair of tens. If he did not place a pair or higher denomination chips on or under a stack, but dropped a sequence of chips with his left hand, he could indicate ten through Ace. A casual observer would never catch it. In fact, both he and Vivian would have to pay very close attention to avoid missing the pattern.

Paul practiced his system for several hands. When his pocket contained a J and a K, Paul deftly dropped two chips indicating a J, then two more indicating a K. He placed the final chip on the stack of five a fraction of a second later. Paul surmised he and Vivian would have to practice quite a while to get the hang of it. For the present, however, nobody who was watching him 'nervously' playing with his chips had a clue.

Paul continued to practice his chip shuffling for another four hours of play before hunger pangs got to him. He could eat tableside, but he needed to stretch and have a leisurely cigarette. Counting his chips, he found he was ahead by $600. But was he really prepared to cheat like this in a tournament that should be a test of his skill? Was protecting a woman he had really never even met worth this?

Grabbing a roast beef sandwich at the café, Paul wandered into the casino and took a seat at empty Keno machine. There were several other players including a couple of "blue hairs," Paul's term for older women that seemed to be able to sit for hours at slot machines. Probably widows he thought.

His favorite cocktailer, Lisa, arrived just as he put a couple hundred dollars in the machine.

"Hi Paul, it's nice to see you again so soon," she said cheerfully, clearly not at all put off by the fact that he had stood for the purpose of looking down the deeply cut front of her uniform. "How's the luck?"

"Pretty good," he told her. "I just took a break to eat, play some Keno, and get a drink. You look terrific as usual. Still married?"

"Yes, still married, but like I've always told you, you'll be the first to know if I'm not."

"Well, maybe I can't wait. You're breaking my heart now!" What time do you get off?" he added, only half-kidding.

"In an hour," she said with a seriousness that took him by surprise. "I can't hang out here. Against the rules, you know. How about we meet at Montblue for a harmless drink? I have time."

"Terrific!" Paul said. "Harmless it will be. I heard the bar there had improved since Caesars sold it. Meet you at the main bar in an hour?"

Lisa looked at her watch, "That will be great, but I can only stay for one drink. What can I bring you now?"

"Bring me a gin and tonic please, Lisa," He told her grinning. "I promise I won't get too far ahead of you."

"I'll be right back," Lisa said, and then as an afterthought, "You are here alone this time aren't you?"

"Of course, I am." Paul said indignantly, surprised to find that it upset him that she should think that he was the sort of man who was always with different women. Because that was what she implied. He supposed that, according to a lot of people, he *was* a womanizer. But there was more to him that that now. Vivian had brought him to that realization. He needed her. He knew that now. And that meant he had to do whatever it took to keep her from becoming criminally involved with RJ.

It had turned cold and the wind whipped through his thin shirt as Paul walked the short distance to Montbleu, mentally ticking off his schedule for the rest of the evening. He had to call Vivian, read some key chapters of his better poker books, try to memorize poker odds tables; and play poker for at least another hour or two. The drink with Lisa wouldn't take too long, although maybe it would be more than a drink. Naw! He shook off the thought and continued on to the main bar at Caesars. After all, he had more important things to think about and do. There might have been a time when he would have had to bedded Lisa to prove a point if for no other reason. But not any more.

"Hi Paul, you don't have a drink yet?" Lisa said ten minutes later while he was concentrating on the game menu of the slot machine set in the bar top.

"He's just bringing it now. What will you have?" Paul said easing off his bar stool, and assisted Lisa onto hers. He had never seen her out of uniform before and she was appealing in a girlish way, dressed in jeans and a sweatshirt. In her cocktailer uniform, Lisa certainly showed she was well endowed. Now, her baggy sweatshirt did its best to hide those features. Still, she was strikingly beautiful and it appeared to Paul that she might be part Filipino or Hawaiian.

"Well, I don't usually drink the hard stuff before I go home," she told him, "but I'll have a Bloody Mary."

"Thanks for meeting me," Paul said. "We've never had much of a chance to talk in the casino. What's going on in your life?"

As Lisa told him about her job at Harrah's, her husband, Jim, her attempt at being a ski instructor, bad and good tippers, and various other jobs from her past, while Paul tried to keep from thinking about all he had to do. Besides talking about his poker tournament in Vegas next week, the only personal information Paul shared was about his career path from California, to Illinois to Sacramento, only briefly mentioning his two ex-wives.

After Lisa left to go home, Paul slouched back to Harrah's scolding himself repeatedly for having taken the time from poker to talk to Lisa even though he had enjoyed himself. His weakness for women was taking its toll. A sudden sense of being unsettled came over him. RJ, the tournament, the chip scheme, work issues, the drive to Vegas, Vivian, and Maureen. He felt overwhelmed with everything that was going on right now, until he reminded himself that all he had to do was what he had done in the past, work through the issues one at a time. At the very least he had to get back on track with Vegas, the potential 'plot,' and Vivian. When he returned to his room, he called her if for no other reason than to remind himself of what an unusual woman she was, a smart, sexy lady who was still going to bring the kind of excitement he hadn't known for a long time back into his life. If he could keep her from becoming a criminal, that is.

Returning to the poker room, he concentrated on his game, and manipulating his chips. Although the play was unexciting and the other players boring, the evening passed with Paul winning an additional $700. Before he turned in for the night, he had the satisfaction of knowing he had played flawlessly. He didn't need to cheat to win.

CHAPTER 11

PAUL HAD A scant three and half days or so to get his job in order, show his young lieutenant, Dave, the ropes, and take care of a myriad of details. He scanned his full calendar on his office computer and discovered that the Monday morning president's staff meeting had been cancelled again, giving him an extra hour to organize and get on with things. He was writing an e-mail when the president, Gary Richmond suddenly appeared without knocking as usual and sat down facing Paul.

After the usual questions about golf and other meaningless odds and ends, Gary said, "Paul, I know you're taking off at the end of the week for ten, well deserved vacation days. But there's a little concern about your department functioning at its best while you are away. We have several clients in the middle of crucial test phases and I have a number of potential customers coming in next week. You know how good you are at selling new clients on implementations, training and such."

Paul had dreaded that they might have this conversation ever since he had asked Gary for the time off. His mind raced at sonic speed trying to formulate a response to Gary's fears.

"The sales team has expressed doubts about Dave covering for you," Gary continued. "They say he just doesn't have your skills at dealing with emergencies and putting potential clients at ease. I told the sales team, I wasn't going to stop you from going on vacation, but that I would talk to you about Dave and how reachable you would be in Las Vegas."

This wasn't an uncommon situation for Paul. For most of his career, he had been the go-to guy and often, when trying to take time off, or groom a subordinate for his replacement, other departments, that depended on Paul, had often tried to delay or cancel his personal plans. He knew he had to do better and positioning his key subordinates, in this case Dave, far earlier in his timeline. As a good company man, always, Paul would never leave his department in incapable hands and it infuriated him that executives failed to see that it him.

"Gary, you know how much I love the company and its potential." Paul said. "I'd never do anything to jeopardize my department's performance in regard to implementing our software and the support it gives sales. Dave is a good man and this will help him grow, but damn, Gary, those sales people are paranoid. And I..."

Gary interrupted him with a wave of his hand. "Paul, you don't need to say anything. I trust you and your decisions." He winked. "I told sales I would talk to you and I have. Have a great time. I'll probably see you before you leave."

Gary started to leave and then turned back.

"And good luck in Vegas, he said. "Incidentally, you'll have your cell phone with you won't you? Oh, and by the way, can you make a meeting in the main conference room Thursday morning at nine? I'd like to go over a few things."

"Sure thing," Paul replied, wondering what they would be. With that, Gary left Paul's office.

Gary was a whiz at running the company; Paul reflected when he was gone. Mostly a hands-off kind of guy as long as you performed. He imagined Gary would probably tell sales something like, "I told Paul that if anything went wrong while he was gone he would have to answer to me!"

Paul was about to turn back to his computer screen when Maureen appeared in his doorway. "How was the weekend with Fred?" she asked him.

"Hi Maureen. Just great. Great. We went for a drive, ended up in Tahoe, and did some gambling again."

He was beginning to hate all this lying. For a moment when Maureen had mentioned Fred, he couldn't think whom she was talking about. Maureen thought he was with an old friend. Vivian thought he was at a company conference. It was all getting too much. Too complicated.

"You look very nice today," he told her, happy to change the subject.

Maureen grinned. "My mom and I took the kids shopping and I spent some of my winnings on new clothes and some toys. I also bought a couple of new suits for work." She pirouetted like a model, showing off a navy blue knit suit that fitted her like a glove.

"Did you and Fred win?" she asked playfully.

Paul told her, "Fred's not much of a gambler, but was happy to play quarters for a while, while I played some Hold'em. I did pretty well. Final tune-up for Vegas you know."

"Oh God, don't remind me," Maureen told him. "Are we going to have a chance to get together before you leave? My mom's free to watch the kids every night except Wednesday."

Paul hesitated a moment. "Maureen," he said finally, "you know I'd love to, but Gary just left my office and I need to get a bunch of things done before he'll let me leave on vacation. I need to spend quite a bit of time on them tonight and Tuesday working at home where I won't be interrupted."

Maureen frowned, "I saw Gary leave your office and wondered what that was about." She brightened. "You still have to eat, don't you? I could come over late. Bring a pizza or something. I promise not be a distraction. Not for too long, that is."

Maureen had that 'I won't be denied look,' that Paul was becoming all too familiar with. What the hell, Paul thought. If he worked things right, she be in and out in an hour and half, max.

After Maureen left, Paul leaned back in his chair and stared into space, hoping he wouldn't be interrupted for a few more minutes as he sorted out the next several days. Hard work today, tonight, and tomorrow and Maureen tomorrow night. A call to Vivian after sex with Maureen. Work on Tuesday. Work on Wednesday. Pack and load his car Wednesday night. Ready for a departure to Vegas, hopefully not too late Thursday afternoon.

During his drive home that Monday evening, he felt exhausted. And Maureen was coming over tomorrow night, more than likely, expecting sex. Hell, he thought. He'd work hard Wednesday and most of Thursday, and drive nearly halfway to Vegas Thursday night so that he could arrive in Vegas about midday Friday. Then Vivian would arrive later in the afternoon. The odds were great that they would have sex shortly after that. And, how he did like having great odds. He felt a twinge of desire surge through him as he thought about Vivian. But would he have enough energy left to please her on Friday?

Interesting, he thought. Maureen was coming over tomorrow night and he really liked her, but the thought of Vivian stirred him more. Was it because he had not yet met Vivian, and Maureen and he had already been intimate several times? No, it was more than that. The sense of freedom that Vivian brought with her was something that he had to hold onto. At least for now, even though he was not really certain what it all meant.

That evening, Vivian answered Paul's call with, "Hi Paul, only four days left."

"Hi yourself, my dear lady. Actually, it's only about ninety-six hours. More like less than seventy-two hours until I start driving to Vegas. I can't wait, but I have a lot to do before then."

"You poor hardworking executive." Vivian mocked him, "How are they ever going to get along without you?"

"They'll just have to," he told her, only half kidding. "If things go right, I may just never come back. Incidentally, I've thought of a way we can tell one another what we have in the pocket. I'll show you how it works when we meet. For now, all I should say is practice shuffling your chips."

Needing to get off the phone and do some eNovalon work, Paul said his good nights and promised Vivian he would call tomorrow night. Then, remembering Maureen's visit, Paul quickly added that he had a meeting tomorrow night with the president, so he wasn't sure how late it would be before he could call. "Or, I may call you from the office," he added.

Paul's story about his busy schedule seemed to satisfy Vivian, but she made him promise he would call every hour while on the road to Vegas. "I couldn't bear to think about you being in an accident or something," she explained. The request made Paul feel a little uncomfortable and "controlled" but he put that thought aside and said he'd do it for her. After all, she was the woman who was going to help him liberate himself from his, so far, unfulfilled life. The promise of the smart, lively Vivian in his life was paramount.

The next day was hectic and Dave kept interrupting Paul's schedule with questions. Paul sensed he was getting a bit nervous about being in charge, and made sure his quiet coaching encouraged Dave to figure out his own answers.

"Ok Dave, what would you do if I weren't here to answer?" he'd say or "Get used to asking other department manager's your questions as well. Use them as a resource, particularly Maureen; she knows how this place operates. She'll be extremely helpful."

As six o'clock approached, Paul remembered to call Vivian. They talked for about fifteen minutes before Paul announced that he had to go and meet Gary. Then, conferring with Maureen before his drive home, he suggested that she come over at eight-thirty rather than eight because he had a long financial report to write and had the feeling once she came over he would not get back to it. He was right.

Dinner and sex with Maureen that evening seemed very special, perhaps because it would be their last time alone together for almost two weeks, or perhaps because he had an ominous feeling about his caper in Vegas. Hell, unless he was careful to keep both their hands clean in regard to RJ's caper, they might both find themselves behind bars or on the lam. And that was, he thought, more excitement than even Vivian was interested in.

As they basked in the afterglow of their lovemaking, Maureen was the first to speak. "Paul, when you get back, I'd love for you to come over to my house, have dinner and spend some time with my kids. Randy and Chelsea really are good children and I just know that would love you. And you them."

"That's sounds really good Maureen," Paul said, hoping that he sounded sincere, even though he had grave misgivings about her children. "I'll look forward to it."

Actually, his brain was melting down at the thought of Maureen falling in love with him and expecting him to become a stepfather and her devoted husband. If she knew the truth about him, about Vivian and RJ and all the rest, she would probably scramble out of his bed screaming to never see him again.

Paul's next day was as frenzied as usual. Maureen bopped into his office several times, mostly on business, although more than once, she tried to get him to commit to dinner upon his return from Vegas. She also asked, no, begged him to call her when he had breaks in the poker action and made him promise to call often during his drive. Oh Boy! He could just imagine having to call Vivian and then Maureen during his drive. Oh well, he rationalized, at least it would make his drive go by faster. He wrote himself a note listing some things that he had to remember to pack tonight! Vegas inched closer.

After another frozen dinner that evening, Paul completed the important work for eNovalon, including a complicated hourly pricing sheet for the finance department, than he had originally planned. Then, since there was plenty of time to pack, he decided to call Vivian and then do something he not had a chance to do for days, log on to Casinoholdem for one final practice session.

Tapping one foot in time to the raindrops on the roof of his patio, he thought first of Maureen and then of the fiery Vivian. Security. Risk taking. And the problems associated with juggling relationships with two women at the same time. Was it always going to be this way, he wondered? And if it were, would there be any happiness at the end of his particular rainbow? He snuffed out his cigarette and went about his packing.

CHAPTER 12

THURSDAY MORNING CAME soon enough. Get-a-way-day! His car was gassed up and he hoped to be able to hit the road before three or four in the afternoon. Using Mapquest to chart his route, he figured he'd get to at least Fresno and maybe Bakersfield by late evening. The only thing wrong with the BMW was that it wasn't equipped with a navigation system. It served his impulse-buying-ass right that he hadn't even been able to wait a week for the dealer to get another BMW with the NAV System.

Settling into his office chair, Paul fired up his computer. He pulled up his schedule and the list of reminders and noted that there was nothing left to do except attend Gary's meeting at nine and spend an hour with Dave at two to go over last minute details. After preparing his out-of-office reply for his e-mail, he sent out his cell phone number to his staff and the other senior executives for use only in emergencies. Underlining, bolding and italicizing emergencies for emphasis. As for the e-mail, he had cleaned it up last night, now however, there was a new entry from Maureen, titled Lunch?

Good morning, Paul,

I know you will be busy getting ready to leave today – I will sure miss you – but thought maybe we could have lunch if you can squeeze it in. I have a busy day as well, but am open from 11:30 to 1:30, so if you can make an hour during that time, I would really like it. Lunch will be on me!

M.

"I'll pick the most expensive restaurant in town," he kidded her, in his reply thinking he felt like shit, as she clearly liked him and knew at sometime soon, he'd drop her on her head.

His computer reminder chimed promptly at two minutes before nine. The office was amazingly quiet as Paul picked up his note pad and headed to the main conference room, wondering what Gary had in mind in the way of going over client details. When he opened the door to the large conference room, he was rocked back by a loud, "Surprise!"

Seventy-five employees squeezed into the room, many of them standing at the end of the large conference table on which was set a huge sheet cake, with paper plates, forks, and napkins stacked neatly beside it. "Good Luck, Paul," was scripted on the cake in chocolate frosting, surrounded by the images of poker cards.

"What's all this?" was all Paul could muster, aware that he was flushing. The crowd broke into a cacophony of, "Good luck," "We'll be thinking of you," and "Take their money!"

Paul had just started shaking hands and giving a million thank-yous to his well-wishers, when somebody began taking pictures of him and Maureen who was hovering near. Two of the accounting women started cutting the cake, in assembly line fashion, one of them handing Paul the first piece, a large one.

Gary finally got the attention of the gathering and started his speech, "Paul, as you certainly should be able to tell, given the turnout today, you're well liked here at eNovalon. We're lucky to have you as key member of the team and want you to know that we appreciate your hard work. We also want you to know that we would like you to just concentrate on winning in Las Vegas. Try not to think about this place too much. You've earned your time off. Good luck from all of us."

Everyone clapped as Gary shook Paul's hand. "Paul," he added, looking pointedly at Ted Jones, Director of Sales, "if any of my staff has to call you while you're away, they'll have to answer to me."

Paul was unexpectedly touched by this display of affection.

"You mean we're not going over the backup plans to use during my absence, Gary?" he said, grinning as everyone laughed. "I hardly know what to say. I look around the room and see you all as friends. Isn't this a great place to work? And I just have to say how much I appreciate this send-off. If I do really well in Vegas, I'll just have to buy lunch for everyone when I get back. Well, maybe I'll buy lunch no matter what happens. I love you all! Thanks again. Let's eat the cake."

As his fellow employees broke in to little groups, Maureen took Paul's arm, "You have to take me to lunch when you get back," she murmured. "before you buy *everyone* lunch! Are we still on for noon today?"

Actually, their lunch was more of a working lunch than Paul had anticipated. Maureen brought a note pad and asked Paul for the status on several of his staff's client projects that varied from training, implementations, technical assistance, and manual writing.

"There," Maureen said when she was finished. "Now I won't have to call you on business and get into trouble with Gary. It will be just social calls."

The rest of the day went by easily enough. His briefing with Dave went so well, that Paul was confident that his department was safe with the young man at the helm. As promised, he called Maureen to say goodbye just before heading out for his drive to Vegas.

"Wow, you are leaving now," Maureen said. "Can I walk you to the car?" Maureen asked on the phone.

"Sure thing," he told her. "I'm headed that way, right now!"

Paul left a message on his voice mail referring callers to David. After Maureen and Paul had kissed a passionate goodbye behind a Suburban, Paul got in his BMW-750i, and saw her turn to wave, one more time before going inside. Plugging in his radar detector, Paul set his stereo system to the sounds of Bob Florence, and headed out, thinking that Maureen was really something, even if she was a little demanding!

When he was ten miles from Bakersfield, Paul made another of his duty calls to the tired, but wide-awake, Vivian. By the time the odometer had clicked off nearly three hundred miles, he was feeling so drained that he decided to find a place in Bakersfield to stay overnight before pushing on to Vegas early in the morning. Which would allow him to arrive before noon the next day, assuming he got the early start he planned.

His dinner at a Bennigans'was just passable, but it was conveniently next to his motel. Even though it was late in Rockford, he called Vivian once more, as promised, had a final cigarette, set the sleep timer on the TV, and fell asleep, wondering how he and Vivian would hit it off and just how much she was about to complicate his life.

Paul headed south after breakfast, the CD changer loaded with classical music, and gas enough to get him within a hundred miles of Vegas. Interesting he thought. He was just less than three-hundred miles from Vegas, and Vivian about a thousand, but he would only beat her there by a few hours.

Thoughts of Vivian had his mind segueing to the caper. The caper and that character, RJ. Could he trust him? What was the plan? Mulling over all the possibilities in his mind repeatedly, he finally concluded he would at least go through the part about listening to the plan if for nothing but to please Vivian. Besides, he had to know what RJ was up to in order to protect her from herself.

As the now brown countryside of California's central valley opened up in front of him, he speed dialed Maureen's work number and told her he was on his way again after getting a good night's rest.

"Oh Paul," she replied. "I miss you already and I worried about you all night. I know it's silly, but you can't keep the heart and mind quiet when they have so much to say and think about."

Oh Boy, thought Paul. He and Maureen were good friends, both professionally and personally. But now that they had had sex - and granted it had been great sex - Paul admitted to himself, that she was becoming demanding, and rather manipulative.

Maureen caught him up on some business matters and then scolded herself for doing so when he was supposed to be on vacation. Paul had rehearsed his next line.

"Maureen," he said. "I reviewed the tournament schedule in my room last night, and assuming that I'm going to playing well each day, I'm not going to have much time to call you, if at all. Of course I'll try, but I just thought I'd let you know, that it looks like I'm not going to have much spare time."

"I understand Paul," she said, unremittingly cheerful as usual. "But you could call just before you go to bed each night. I know they let you sleep each night, don't they?"

His heart dropped. That was exactly the kind of response he had been afraid she would come up with.

"Of course they let us sleep," Paul said, continuing to follow his internal script. "But it might not be but just a few hours, depending on the round and players left to be eliminated. But I promise to try."

Incredibly enough, Maureen, would not let up. "I know you'll *try*," she said. "And I know you'll miss me too much to not to call, even it it's only for a minute."

In the end, he signed off with the promise to call when he arrived safely in Vegas.

Damn Maureen, he thought. He pictured himself grabbing his cell phone when Vivian wasn't around or other spare time to call her. He then realized that if he didn't call her, she would attempt to call him in his room. Shit, had he told her where he was staying? He couldn't remember for sure, but would be surprised if he hadn't since she hadn't asked. Then again, perhaps she thought his cell phone number was all she needed. He'd have to keep it off when he wasn't using it. Be careful, Langley, he thought.

As the miles sped by, Paul continued to think about the complicated web he was weaving, to the sound of Lennie Neihaus' great dance charts for Stan Kenton. Vivian and Maureen. Two special women each in their own way. And RJ's plot. Life had been easier when he was married. At least his girl friends then had known that it was necessary to cover his tracks now and then. He smiled as he thought how many times he had seen this play out in the movies. The trouble was that, in films, one of the women always caught the male character. He would have to be careful.

At about a hundred miles from Vegas, he pulled into a Chevron service station to fill his fuel tank and empty his bladder. After he paid for the gas and a bag of Fritos, he sat on a bench outside and had a cigarette. It was definitely warmer in this part of the country, he thought as he looked at the sparse brush and cacti scattered about on the high desert countryside. He looked at the bugs smeared on the BMW's grill and headlights as he contemplated the quick life of some creatures. Was it true some insects only lived for a day? He read that somewhere. He wondered how a twenty-four hour period passed for an insect. Birth. Sex. College. Kids. Old age. Unless, of course, the poor bugger met a BMW speeding along the highway. Life is mysterious all right he thought, and his life is an even bigger one!

Paul settled into his car and started off, estimating that it was only about two or so hours to Vegas. Seeing that he had missed a call on his phone, Paul punched up his voice mailbox as he accelerated the BMW up the on-ramp to Interstate 15. It was Vivian calling from O'Hare just before boarding.

"You must have been in a dead cell area," she said, or on the side of the road relieving yourself!" She said. "At least I hope it's nothing worse than that. I have to turn off my cell now, so the next time we talk I will be in Vegas. Drive safely. I can't wait."

The speed-o-meter was running over 80mph, but he was staying with the flow of traffic that was heavy enough so that setting the cruise control was more of a hassle that it was worth. He would turn the Sinatra CD, *The Very Good Years at Reprise*, up to blast level and sing along to, *Luck Be a Lady* when he crossed the state line into Nevada! He was ready to have some luck and that included doing whatever had to be done to keep Vivian from going at it alone with RJ's caper.

He found himself examining his feelings about Vivian and Maureen, in that order. He really cared for Maureen but Vivian was the extraordinary kind of women he had dreamed of, with a body that seemed built for lovemaking, and intelligent enough to carry on great conversations on nearly any subject. Moreover, she had a wild side, almost a devil-may-care one that frightened and excited him at the same time. The word, love entered his mind again.

He thought of Helen and his lustful beginnings with her when he was married to Shasta. She had been exciting all right, but he still hadn't had that feeling of unconditional love that he wanted so much to feel. The only time in his life he felt that way, was a crush he had on a girl at his junior high School. He remembered not being able to sleep, eat or anything. She consumed his entire being. Paul remembered his grandmother, pooh-poohing his listlessness. "Paul, you're only fourteen years old. It's just puppy love!" Puppy love might have been right, but he had never felt like that about another woman again. He was still searching.

When Paul crossed the Nevada state line at Primm, he pulled into a casino to get some chocolate, have a cigarette and to stretch his legs. He had plenty of time to get to the Four Queens, check-in and maybe even take a short nap before Vivian arrived. He would have to be alert when he met RJ later tonight.

"Luck be a lady, tonight," Paul bellowed, as he started the short remaining desert trek to Vegas. He was sure he sang off key, but

Frank would never know. He grinned. What a great swinging arrangement by Billy May.

He called Maureen as the city of Vegas came into view.

"Hi Hon, I'm almost there," he told her. "I can see the casinos on the strip and the Stratosphere tower. I should be in my room with in the hour. I even stopped in Primm for a smoke and a stretch. Played video poker for about fifteen minutes and came out fifty dollars ahead."

"Perhaps you should turn around and come home now that you're ahead!" Maureen told him and for a moment, he was not sure whether or not she was joking.

CHAPTER 13

AS THE FOUR Queens parking attendant drove off with Paul's car after promising to get it washed, the bellman loaded Paul's luggage and boxes onto a cart. For some reason, Paul felt amazingly cool, even though the air was warm, but Paul was cool even though he was a bit uneasy about meeting Vivian in the flesh, even if he ignored the fact that, via RJ, she might well be leading him into a corner he would find difficult to get out of. When he added Vivian's name as an occupant in his room, the desk clerk gave him *that* look and a crooked smile. Paul was thinking it was a good thing that Vegas lived by its motto: "Things that happen in Vegas stay in Vegas."

The long drive would have normally tired him out, but now that he was here, he felt miraculously revived. Vivian's flight from Chicago wasn't due to arrive for about two hours. Although they had certainly been intimate via e-mails, pictures and phone calls, he was still concerned that they might not hit it off despite their shared hedonistic instincts. Everything had to be perfect.

After ordering some additional wine and soft drinks for the little hotel refrigerator, Paul set out the two decks of cards, box of chips, and his CD player. Moving the thermostat up past the current setting of "freezing," he took a quick freshen-up shower and then sprawling on the bed nude, set the alarm for forty-five minutes, and tried to doze off, although the thoughts of Vivian, RJ, and Maureen kept him from relaxing completely.

When it was time to dress, he decided on wearing his silk boxers since they were less restrictive and under certain circumstances more revealing. Next, he put on black slacks and a dark blue golf shirt. Pretty casual, but this was Vegas. Inspecting himself in the mirror, he decided that he was ready to rendezvous at Hugo's Cellar, one of the great places to eat in downtown Vegas.

Realizing that Vivian's flight should have landed a few minutes ago, Paul punched in her cell phone number hoping, she had turned it on as promised as soon as the plane touched down.

"Hello," Vivian answered, her voice garbled a bit, but still sultry. *He'd like to wring the neck of that 'can you hear me now' character.*

"Hi, and let me be the first to welcome you to Las Vegas," Paul replied. "Looks like you're right on time."

Vivian sounded excited. "Where are you now?"

"In our room," Paul said. "making sure everything is just right."

"I can't wait. Do you still want to meet in the restaurant first? What should I do with my luggage?"

"When you arrive have the bellman deliver it to 609." Paul told her. That's the closest I could get to your favorite number."

After they agreed to meet at Hugo's, Paul loaded Ravel's *Bolero* in his CD player and set the timer to start playing in two and half hours. Playing *Bolero* during sex may be a clichéd thing to do, but with his and Vivian's musical tastes being so aligned, Paul thought it would be the right thing to do. After one more check of the room, he wandered around the Four Queen's casino, getting the lay of the land. It was much smaller than he had imagined with the machines placed much closer together than they were in some of the larger casinos he'd visited. The anteroom to the tournament was set up for registration and the ESPN TV crews were busy pulling cable and organizing boxes of equipment that were stacked in the wide hallway. The sign at the entrance was a duplicate of the one hanging at the entrance to the hotel, red lettering on white satin: 'Four Queen's First Annual Big Stakes Texas Hold'em Poker Tournament.' In smaller print it read, "Cash prizes totaling **TWO MILLION DOLLARS!**" Paul's heart skipped a beat.

An armed guard was standing at the entrance to the temporary poker room and Paul approached him to ask if he could peek in. "Not unless you have one of these," The man said, pointing to the pass hanging around his neck. "Security and TV crews are the only ones allowed in the room right now. It will open in the morning. You playing?"

"Yes," Paul told him. "Thought I'd just see how it was set-up, but I can wait. Thanks"

"Good luck," said the guard as Paul turned to explore the rest of the area.

After trying to calm his nerves by playing a bit of Keno, Paul descended the dozen or so stairs to the restaurant and arrived in a world far removed from the casino. Miraculously, the lights and noises just above disappeared completely. Intimacy and casual elegance greeted him as he passed the small bar. The brick walls, adorned with art provided an ambience that Paul had not quite expected. The restaurant atmosphere was inviting, with warmth not often found in Vegas' eateries. Hugo's radiated a touch of class, from the carpet, table settings, and the formally dressed wait staff and hostess. Following the Maitre'd to his table, Paul noted several tuxedo clad waiters, attentively bending over tables taking orders or mixing salads in large bowls with flourishes that would envy Toscanini. The few patrons were casually dressed and neat. Paul fit in perfectly. The setting was ideal for their first meeting.

The maitre'd soon arrived with a stunning redhead in tow, holding her complimentary rose. Paul watched the other men's heads swivel as their eyes followed Vivian in her progress to his table. Paul rose. Their eyes met, and sparks started to fly.

Vivian was as alluring as her internet pictures had promised. She was dressed perfectly for the occasion in form fitting black slacks, and a red halter-top that revealed her ample cleavage between the lapels of her loosely fit white linen jacket. They stared into each other for what seemed a long time, her green eyes piercing his soul, although all Vivian could muster was, "Oh you're even taller than I imagined."

When Paul kissed her lightly on the cheek, she said with a smile, "We can do better than that, how about a hug!"

"Let's do even better," Paul told her, leaning down to kiss her.

Slowly. He made their first kiss slow, gentle, and easy. What passed between them was a cauldron of seething desire. Vivian's lips melted into his. It was delicious.

This time, all Vivian could muster was, "Wow. Thanks. Nice."

After Paul ordered two martinis, just the way they both liked them - Blue Sapphire gin, olives, twist and slightly dirty - they began to talk as if they had known each other forever, about books, politics, music, world affairs, everything and anything. Vivian also displayed her financial planning expertise, commenting on the state of the stock market, world bond market and living trusts. Paul was delighted to find her as compatible and as intelligent as she had appeared on line and their many phone conversations.

When Paul started to ask her about RJ, however, Vivian looked about the room and shushed him. "Let's not talk about him or that now," she said in a low voice. "Let's talk about us."

For a moment, when she said that, Paul allowed himself to have hope that she had decided not to try her hand at criminal activity after all. It occurred to him that if he could prove to her that their relationship could be exciting with out the added kick that a "caper" might provide, he could forget about the RJ problem/

For dinner, they both decided on the Lobster Bisque as a starter, followed by a spectacular salad made tableside by an attentive staff member. After that, they each decided on the *Scallops Orange Beurre Blanc*, translated into Pan seared scallops with a tangy reduction of fresh orange juice finished with butter. The food was indeed a culinary delight, but their minds were not on their food.

"You're more beautiful than your pictures," Paul told her unable to decide whether to look into those enticing green eyes or admire her cleavage. Electricity was starting to flow, both of them fully aware that they would soon be upstairs fulfilling all their e-mail and phone call fantasies.

Over Kahlua and coffee, Vivian became very bold, moving her hand up Paul's thigh and wrapping her fingers around his genitals. "Oh yum, Paul," she said. "You are definitely a handful!"

Paul found that he was enjoying the hell out of Vivian. Her slightly crooked smile, the way she talked, her boldness, her cleavage. He couldn't wait to explore every single square centimeter of her.

Paul signed the check and they went to find their room, holding hands.

Soon they were in the semi-dark room and kissing deeply as Paul pulled her into him, feeling the smooth skin of her back under her halter-top. He filled his hands with her marvelous breast, her nipples pressing against his palms. Vivian moaned with pleasure, rubbing the length of his shaft through his pants, as he removed her halter-top and buried his face between her breasts.

"Oh Paul, this is going to be so wonderful," Vivian said breathlessly.

Just as he pulled off his shirt and threw it aside, the familiar strains of the Bolero started softly. "Oh my God, Paul!" Vivian exclaimed. "What perfect music. I love it."

As he nibbled and licked her free-swinging breasts, she fumbled with his belt and fly. When she had pushed his pants down past his modest love handles, Paul heard her gasp.

His penis swung free now and she grasped it with an adept hand. Paul let out his breath and moaned at the wonderful feeling of her holding him. Hooking his fingers into her slacks and panties, he pushed them down, rubbing his erection against her thigh as they fell onto the bed. His mouth hungry against hers, he moaned as he pressed his hardness against her warm thighs, luxuriating in her soft skin, and her breasts, cresting and so full that he could not resist losing himself in each of them, in turn. He loved the thrill that raced through him as his tongue played at her nipples, driving her insane with pleasure. She signaled him, pushing him to explore further, to travel down her body. Paul became even harder for her, and her sighs filled the air. He expertly placed his tongue against her there, gently, and carefully.

Her thighs alternately tightened and relaxed their grip on his head as he eagerly lapped and nibbled, her moans and sighs giving him all the encouragement he needed to keep going. As the music grew louder , her hips and thighs moved against him in rhythm until, after several minutes, Paul could feel her orgasm start as he intensified his lapping around her now swollen clitoris. Vivian's juices were really flowing as her thighs gripped his head in the throes of her climax.

"Put it in me now," Vivian groaned as Paul placed the head of his thickness in her sweet opening. "But, God, Paul, please go slow!"

He inched his thickness inside her in several slow, ever penetrating moves, and then all the way in. "Oh! Oh! Yes! Yes!" they cried out in unison as he plunged in and out of her, changing the length and frequency of each thrust. He sensed Vivian was going to come again! In this position, he could kiss her sweet, soft lips again. His own volcanic eruption delayed, was now screaming to happen.

Wanting her to be on top, so that his hands could fill themselves with her pendulous breasts as his thickness rode up, deep inside her, he deftly moved her over him, his hands tight around her waist. Vivian moved down on him, impaling herself even deeper. Her head arched back as his hands pressed against the wonderfully full melons of her breasts.

The music was reaching its final strains, carrying them away with all their passion, and pleasure.

Paul's own orgasm started in the small of his back and quickly moved to the front of him. He could not have stopped it now in any way. The inevitable charging inside Vivian continued as he flexed his body in anticipation of the impending explosion. Her legs squeezed him as he pushed even deeper. Their moans and sighs grew louder, in unison as his culmination moved to his balls and charged up the length of his buried shaft. "Oh God!" he shouted as he pumped inside her as they climaxed at the same time.

The music ended at that moment as if a movie score had been playing, crashing to an ending just as they finished. They lay entwined, Vivian sprawled against his chest, while he remained large, still inside her, drenched in sweat, feeling the marvelous afterglow together.

"Whew. I feel so empty now," Vivian told him, snuggling by his side, "but at the same time so complete."

Vivian leaning over to get a cigarette exposed her near perfect back and a beautiful tattoo of an antique jeweled broach at the base of her spine. "Oh God this is so good," she said as she lit two cigarettes and gave one to him. "Life is perfect. I just love sex so much and, you my big man! God! What a wonderful lover. I'd have to put you among my top five."

"What a pair we are," Paul told her. "It's as if we were made for each other. Incidentally, I want to examine that gorgeous tattoo on your back sometime, sometime very soon."

Until they had had begun to make love, Paul had not realized how distracted he had been by the business with RJ, but now he felt so complete, so satisfied. Had he met his soul mate? If so, it was more important than he thought to keep her from putting herself in danger by associating with RJ.

"Have you heard from RJ?" Paul said, trying to sound casual. "I haven't."

"Nope. I sure haven't," Vivian said, "I was going to ask you about the signaling scheme you came up with. How does it work?"

"Now hear me out on this," Paul said, "Look, we're both really good players and cheating is not going to do anything, but perhaps get us into a lot of trouble, and frankly, for me, cheating at the game

I so dearly love, well, it's just not right. I want us to succeed in this tournament, without any gimmicks. Let's show the world how good we are without cheating."

Paul hoped he wouldn't have to do this as a distraction from her penchant to play in RJ's plot.

"I guess I can't disagree with that," Vivian agreed. "But what about RJ's requirement for us to get to the final table? Based on what you said he said, isn't it really important for the heist?"

Shit, she's still serious! Ok, Paul thought, the best way to handle this it seemed, was to pretend to go along with her for now, until he could think of a way out. A way out for her.

"That may be *his* requirement," Paul said, "But it's certainly not *mine*, at least not until we've heard his plan. We may just not participate, if it's too risky for us. I'd still rather not cheat; even if it turns out to be paramount we make it to the table."

"Do you have any idea what he has in mind?" Vivian asked. "I've been thinking about all that money lying on the table in full view of security, TV cameras, and the crowd. It's hard to imagine what he's thinking, but it's still so exciting. Don't you at least agree with that? Think of the thrill, Paul. If you thought the sex was good just now, can you imagine how exciting it will be…"

"Yes, it's exciting all right, but it's nerve racking too," he interrupted her. "I've been thinking about his potential plan as well. Maybe he wants to take it during its transit in or out of the room. I don't really know. I guess if I were planning it, I'd have to know a lot more about where the money comes from, how many men are going to be guarding it, and how we're supposed to get out of the hotel. Getting out of downtown would be hard enough with all the surveillance cameras and such. I just don't know. I think I'm more worried about our role in this and finding out for sure, why we need to get to the final table. Maybe he'll tell us tonight, that it can't be done."

"Oh no Paul," Vivian said in a matter of fact voice. "I am sure he has a plan."

Tangling themselves together in a companionable silence, they relaxed in each other's embrace. Still, Paul's mind kept racing with thoughts of the meeting with RJ. The time they spent lying there together passed as swiftly as a dream and Paul was comforted by the warmth of her and the sound of her soft breathing.

When Paul and Vivian finally looked at the clock, they discovered that they had less than two hours to get over to Cashman field to rendezvous with RJ.

"Paul." Vivian started. "I've been thinking and I think you're right about cheating at cards. We shouldn't do it. That does sound strange, when we're about to hear about a plot to *steal* two million dollars, but let's at least hear his plan. And will you show me chip scheme anyway? After all, you probably went to a lot of trouble to work it out."

Good sign, Paul thought, Vivian thinks we shouldn't cheat either. Maybe she'll also draw the line at theft. Was she just saying this or was her motive something else?

Vivian caught on to his chip handling very quickly. Vivian would read his pocket cards. Then she would do the same all without either of them actually using a deck. Eventually, Paul broke out the deck, shuffled, and dealt two to Vivian. Playing with her chips, quite expertly, Vivian went through a pattern of 'nothing.' Paul asked, "No cards?"

They practiced until neither one made a mistake, making sure they always looked like they were nervously playing with their chips.

When it was time to go, Vivian changed into jeans and a white blouse and put on high heels, fluffing out her red locks, behind a white sweatband so that her hair looked like it had in the picture of her sitting at her computer, one of the first pictures she had sent him. Suddenly he felt like this was the culmination of a very long relationship. He wasn't sure where it would lead, but he knew that they were so alike in so many ways that it was almost frightening. As soon a she had said they were too skilled to debase the game by cheating, she had understood. Now if he could only play this business with RJ cleverly enough...

"Wow, nice car Paul!" Vivian exclaimed and interrupted his thinking. They climbed in to the BMW. "You buy or lease this?" She rubbed the leather of the armrest.

"I bought it about six months ago. I really like it. It made the drive here very easy."

Jazz piano sounds emanated from the BMW's stereo system as they left the Four Queens. "Oh! Dave Grusin!" Vivian exclaimed. "Mind if I turn that up?"

"We have to talk and I need to concentrate on getting to our rendezvous," Paul told her, switching the music off. "I need to ask you about RJ."

"Tell me how you met and why you broke up? I'm not paranoid - well maybe I am a little - but I'm entering very unfamiliar territory with all this."

"Well, I guess you should know," Vivian said, placing her hand on Paul's thigh, "that the girlfriend I told you about moving to Rockford a few years ago is really my boss too. Sara was the manager of a small bank in Chicago. What I found out later, is that she really worked for RJ. Cloak and dagger stuff. I'm sure what she was doing at the time was money laundering or something of the sort. We met having a cigarette outside in the freezing cold at a Chicago Symphony concert, and we really hit it off. Anyway, to make a long story short, apparently the Feds had started circling her operation and it was making her nervous, so nervous that she told RJ she was going to close the bank. He wasn't very happy, but she closed it even as difficult is to do, what with government charters and legitimate customers. In the end, RJ helped her open a financial planning office in Rockford."

"During this time she introduced me to RJ and he asked me out," Vivian continued. "Sara didn't tell me right away about his background. We liked each other, but we didn't agree philosophically on anything. He was also pretty much of a chauvinist, expecting me to drop what I was doing or just leaving without telling me where or when he might call again. Finally, we decided just to be friends."

"There has to be more than that," Paul protested. "How did you find out he was Mafia? Sara finally tell you? And if you two were getting along so great, why was he willing to give up on you? I'd never let you get away that easy!"

"We really just had different tastes," she said. "He would drag me to all kinds of clubs and concerts that I hated. He knew that, too, but he liked to be out in the public with a redhead on his arm. The term "Mobster Moll" entered my mind from time to time. But what does that matter now? I know you aren't keen about this, but I want to hear what he has planned."

What was she hiding? Paul wondered. Maybe nothing. She's at least agreed that we don't need to cheat, but here we are going to meet her ex-gangster boyfriend, and talk about a major heist. He would certainly keep his wits about him and keep an eye on how RJ and Vivian interact.

They followed the signs to Cashman Center in silence, passing the baseball field with its looming light towers. Wheeling the sedan around to the entrance of the parking lot, Paul pulled up short of the locked gates.

"Shit! It's closed," he exclaimed, while Vivian starring, into the middle distance, said nothing.

This was not a good sign thought Paul as he turned the car around and parked on the busy street across from the field. He looked at his watch: Six minutes before eleven.

"Well, this isn't right. We should be over there, a hundred yards inside the lot."

"Let's try and call RJ," Vivian suggested. "Or perhaps not. He's always running late. Let's stay here a few minutes, and see what happens. Incidentally, does he know what kind of car you have or do you know his?"

"No I don't and he doesn't." Paul said, "All he told me was that you would recognize him when he approached."

"Well, I haven't laid eyes on him in well over a year," Vivian announced, fluffing her hair in animated fashion. "I'm sure he will not have changed much. I certainly haven't."

"Since you're the only one he'd recognize," Paul told her, "why don't you get out of the car and stand over there by the crosswalk before we try and call him. I'll keep an eye on you. If he comes by this way, he should see you there."

After a minute or so, which seemed like an eternity to Paul watching Vivian stand on the corner through his rear view mirror, a car slid to a stop on the corner. It was no surprise to Paul that it was a black, late model Cadillac, had to be a Mafia car. Vivian approached the car, leaned down and spoke into the car. Nodding to the passenger in the back seat, she pointed in Paul's direction and walked back to the BMW.

As Vivian slid into the seat, the Cadillac pulled alongside. "Okay, that's him," Vivian said. "We're to follow him for a bit. He said it wasn't far. About ten minutes."

Paul couldn't see anyone inside through its heavily tinted windows, as he pulled out to follow, he memorized the numbers of the Nevada plates, not sure why.

As they turned south on Casino Center Drive, Paul asked, "Did RJ say anything else?"

"Only, that he was sorry the lot was locked, Vivian told him. "It usually isn't.

She was, Paul thought, unusually distracted. He wondered if seeing RJ again had made her remember the days when they had been close.

They were passing some familiar streets now as they headed east of The Strip: Paradise, Sands Ave., Howard Hughes Parkway. As they moved away from the Strip and downtown, Paul was reminded that Las Vegas was more than casinos and sin. Businesses, schools, churches. Families and large housing developments scattered across the valley floor, bordered by mountains on the north, west, and east side.

If he hadn't known better, Paul might have imagined that Vivian was impatient and annoyed. Certainly, the sultry voice made a disappearance. Not for the first time since he had made her acquaintance, he wondered what in God's name was he doing.

CHAPTER 14

AFTER PASSING SEVERAL business buildings, they turned into an alley somewhere between Howard Hughes Parkway and Paradise crossing a large empty parking lot, and entered a narrow opening at the rear of a two-story office building, surprisingly well lit for a rendezvous like this. The Caddy came to a halt in the parking lot in front of a door marked "Deliveries Only."

Four men emerged from the Caddy, doors opening almost simultaneously, all dressed in dark jackets with open collared shirts. One man was carrying an aluminum briefcase. If, in fact that was RJ, he seemed to be the shortest of the four. Helping Vivian out of the car, Paul, without his jacket, felt underdressed.

One of the men motioned them to the door up the stairs and Paul held Vivian's hand, as one of the men unlocked it. As he and Vivian followed them inside the building, Paul noted that none of these men checked out the area as they entered the building, despite the fact that Paul could almost feel telescopes and night vision cameras clicking away at them from hidden windows. After all this was Vegas and this RJ character and his henchmen might very well be the subject of some federal surveillance. He hoped for his and Vivian's sake that he was wrong.

They walked silently down a long hallway, impressionist prints hung on the walls. Street scenes of Paris, probably. They turned into a conference room decorated with what looked like original oil paintings, on highly polished oak paneling. The few can lights glowing in their recessed holes, reflected on the highly polished surface of the large oak conference table, which was surrounded by plush conference chairs covered in maroon fabric. Not until they circled the table and stood behind the chairs did anyone speak.

As the garish white florescent lights came on overhead, the man, Paul assumed was RJ said, "God, Vivian you look terrific," and hugged her. And then to Paul, "Jeez, you're a tall one. Good goin' Viv.

And you're a short one, thought Paul, although he had to admit that RJ was impeccably dressed in a black suit with a black silk shirt, with a large Rolex on one hairy, bony wrist and a heavy gold bracelet on the other. RJ's eyes, avoided Paul's. He looked a shifty character all right. Why in the world, Paul wondered, had Vivian ever taken up with him?

"I'm sure I am not telling you anything you don't already know," RJ told Paul, still averting his eyes, as they shook hands, "but you are a very lucky man. Vivian is a beautiful, smart lady. I'm sincere when I say that I wish it had worked out between her and me. I hope you treat her right. I hope, for your sake you like classical music."

"Thanks RJ," Vivian said blushing. "Paul is treating me better than you know."

"Yes RJ," Paul added. "I know she's a special lady and yes, we have music as one of our many things in common. We're getting along famously."

RJ introduced the other three other men as, Jamey, Michael, and Alf.

"Jamey and Michael are from Chicago, near me, and Alf lives here in Vegas," he added.

Jamey and Michael, Paul thought, could have passed as brothers. Like RJ, they both had that Italian look. Alf reminded Paul of an auto mechanic that felt a little out of place dressed in his Armani jacket and in an upscale conference room. All of them, including Paul, smiled with their mouths, but not their eyes. They were Paul realized, a breed of men he had never had anything to do with, and he was not at all sure he wanted to start now. It was definitely time to remind himself that he was pretending to go along with this to protect Vivian.

"I'm not going to perform a search for any recording devices," RJ said as they took their seats around the table, "but I assure you both, if you had one, our detectors ..." RJ pointed to the ceiling, "would pick them up. Just so you know."

"RJ, why on earth would you think we're recording this," Vivian said, "Shame on you."

"I'm just a very careful man," RJ told her. "I haven't seen you in over a year and I'm meeting this guy for the first time. I trust you, but, what about a drink? The only thing I can offer you is water at this time of night. Anybody want one? Alf, get us a few bottles and some ashtrays."

Paul was glad to hear they could light up. He was, he found, very nervous. Vivian on the other hand, was sitting straight up, paying attention to everything and didn't appear to be at all apprehensive.

"Okay," began RJ, "I'd like to ask you some questions, Paul. Vivian told me a little about you and I did some checking too. Married twice. Both ex's still living. Shasta remarried and living in Lodi, California. Helen remarried, and divorced. Living in Redondo Beach."

It was news to Paul that Helen had divorced again. But he remained silent. He had a feeling that the less he had to say, the better. After all, he was here to learn all he could about what RJ had in mind.

"You are a high level executive," RJ continued, "Good salary. Good stock options with eNovalon. Comfortable home in a nice area. No outstanding bills. A very decent savings account and investment portfolio. Nice and clean. No arrests other that the usual speeding tickets over the past ten or twelve years"

Paul felt extremely uncomfortable as RJ ticked off these items. It occurred to him to wonder what Vivian had told him versus what he found out on his own.

As if confirming his fears, RJ went on, "You have four bank accounts and pay your bills on-line," RJ said, which answered one question since Paul had not told Vivian about his banking affairs. He hoped that RJ's reach into his personal life had not included RJ's men having him followed to Tahoe last weekend, when Vivian had thought that he was at a company conference! He silently hoped RJ was through.

RJ leaned back in his seat. "So I have one question, Paul. Well actually it's for you, too, Vivian. But Paul, you should answer first. Why would you want to be involved in a potential crime like this? You seem to have everything you need or want for a man of nearly fifty."

Alf returned with the water bottles and ashtrays, announcing, "They're clean." By which Paul assumed that he meant the 'bug detectors' in the ceiling.

"I've been thinking about that question for several weeks now," Paul said, unscrewing the cap and taking a long gulp of water. "I suppose my reasons are complex. Hell, it may take a shrink to figure it out."

"Go ahead." urged RJ.

Time to try to reassure this man enough so that he'd feel free to relieve the details of his plan and hope to hell it would be risky enough to scare Vivian off.

"I hardly know where to begin," Paul told RJ, "I've always had a larcenous side most of my life, with little chance to explore it. True, I've worked hard, kept clean, and done pretty well, in spite of costly divorces. I'm a fan of books and movies about theft and always imagine myself in the middle of all that. I think a part of keeping this on my dark side, so to speak, is that my previous relationships were with women, particularly both wives, which would have gone nuts if I revealed to them I would like to rob a bank, embezzle money, or knock off an armored car."

Now should he implicate Vivian in all this, thought Paul, or let her take a backseat?

As if answering his silent question, Vivian announced, "I won't go nuts. "On the contrary, Paul and I have this in common and stop questioning our motives. We think it's very exciting and the reward could be very nice. Get on with the details, RJ!"

"The important thing is that I'm ready to do this," Paul chimed in, "and am really anxious to hear the details, too."

"Ok, we have desire and opportunity," RJ said, his cigarette ash flying about, as he used his arms in animated fashion. "Now listen to me. There are two key ingredients to committing a crime. First, let's talk about the reward. We figure the cash take of unmarked un-serialized one-hundred dollar bills will equal one point nine million dollars. Reliable sources tell us that the Four Queens will indeed place all the prize money on the awards table next to the final table. Given our expenses, the number of participants on the team and the risks we're taking, we are going to let you and Vivian split thirty percent of the take."

Paul quickly calculated his and Vivian's share would be almost $600k. Would that be more money than she could resist? He glanced at her and saw that her face was expressionless. Was she, he wondered, waiting for him to say something. He tried to think what he would say if he were seriously considering this.

"I don't think that's enough," Paul said. "Particularly since we don't know anything about the plan and the risks we'd need to take. I'm assuming the worst since you told us it was imperative to get to the final table. What if we don't?

"I agree with Paul," Vivian said turning to face RJ directly. "This meeting might as well be over. Come on, Paul. Let's get out of here."

"Fine," RJ said, as Vivian pushed back in her chair. "I think you should hear the plan first and then decide if you want to pass up on an opportunity for six hundred grand."

"Okay, RJ," Vivian said. "Let's hear the plan and then Paul and I can decide if it's worth it or not."

"It had better be good." Paul said, making sure RJ knew he wasn't taking a second seat to Vivian on their reluctance to play.

RJ, who was now looking very tight-jawed about this, the lone black curl on his forehead, jiggling slightly as he held out his hand at Alf and as if he wanted a hit at the blackjack table. Alf slid the briefcase across the table to RJ.

Snapping open the case, RJ pulled out a loosely bound notebook with brads holding the several dozen pages together and he closed the lid, before anyone might have a chance to see the rest of the contents. Paul could see the ESPN logo on the thin cardboard cover before RJ opened the book to the first page.

"Ok," he said, patting the booklet, "We've obtained a lot of information, not only from the ESPN script, but from several inside security sources at the Four Queens. Let me give you an overall idea of how we plan to do this, show you some devices and then we can open it up for questions and further details."

It occurred to Paul to wonder how easy it would be to back out once they had heard the details. Still, it was a risk he had to take. After all, he had to stand beside Vivian all the way now so that he could have the arguments he needed to have to talk her out of taking part in this crazy idea.

"The Four Queens does pretty well in their casino, but since the World Series of Poker left Binions' this year, there is no longer a big tournament downtown. The Four Queens hopes to have this tournament turn into an annual event. Not only have you and Vivian qualified, which makes it seem it was open to the ordinary player, so to speak, they made sure several name players were encouraged to participate as well. They're planning to crank up their marketing."

Paul caught Vivian's eyes and shrugged. So far, what RJ had told them could have been deduced from the material in the tournament letter.

"They are in fact, going to display the cash winnings as advertised," RJ continued, "but they won't bring in the cash until play starts with the seven finalists. ESPN will tape the entire tournament to be broadcast later. Only the final table be will be fitted with cameras to reveal the player's pocket cards. The other twenty or thirty tables will be removed and the audience be allowed a closer look by bringing in additional bleachers and moving the security ropes."

"Come on, RJ, tell us something new," Vivian said, as if reading Paul's mind. "This stuff isn't new."

"Hang on Viv," RJ's dark eyes, narrowed. "The Four Queens doesn't have a lot of space. The remote announcers are being set-up in a room on the second floor. Security is there now running wires from the table to the remote room, so that viewers and commentators can see the cards. The Four Queens has surveillance cameras in the banquet room, but it's all old technology and rarely used. Security will kluge together the cameras and feed the images into their regular observation room. However, most of the cameras are for show. They won't pick up the details of say, a cheating blackjack dealer or a card counter. The room is rarely used for gambling."

As RJ took a long pull on his water, Paul thought, *and not pick-up any chip shuffling scheme.*

"So our plan is that you, whichever one of you at the final table, will have one of these devices."

As RJ pulled out two aluminum cylinders from the briefcase, Vivian said, her voice full of confidence, "We're very good players and Paul and I *will* be at the final table.

The cylinders were about an inch in diameter and almost a foot long with a small protrusion sticking out of the middle. We will go over how you carry these in a bit, but you'll need to place it under your foot and then, at a precise time, push on this button here and kick it to the center of the table." His voice rose a bit, for emphasis, "Without being noticed."

The button, as Paul studied the cylinders, looked, very small, something like a dime, not very well glued or soldered to the side.

"Pushing on the plunger will release a gas that will create a lot of smoke and render whoever breathes it within thirty or forty feet, unconscious for several minutes," RJ said in a not caring-for-life-or-limb manner, as he waved the cylinder around in the air for emphasis. "During the confusion, we'll have several of our men, who will be protected from the affects of the gas, scoop up the money and depart the premises."

"You mean Paul or I will be unconscious too?" Vivian interrupted, as if reading Paul's mind perfectly. "Are you sure this stuff is harmless?"

"Yes," RJ said succinctly, and looked around the room as if waiting for more questions. Jamey and Michael, leaning back in their chairs, looked completely bored. They had, Paul thought, heard all this before. Alf, however, remained upright, his attention riveted on the cylinders.

"Well, what do you think?" RJ asked Paul.

"Man," Paul said, taking in a deep breath. "I have so many questions and that I hardly know where to start. First, as I told you on the phone when all this started, counting on Vivian or me to get to the final table is dicey. What happens if we don't get there?"

"There's a plan B," RJ told him. "We've recruited another player, so the odds of getting one of the three of you to the final table are improved. He's good, and as we know, you and Vivian are, too. I'm not going to tell you who it is, and he won't be told about either of you, for several reasons. One, he has requested we don't tell you who he is, and I assume you wouldn't want him to know about you two either and two, if something goes wrong, the less people know about the identity of other members of our team the better. You can't testify about somebody you don't know. It's protection for all three of you, and two, we thought, could be wrong, but playing each other in the tournament, knowing each other could raise tensions unnecessarily. We also have a more risky plan C. No details for now, but it's riskier because video tapes of the event will be reviewed over and over by the authorities."

"Speaking of video tape," Paul said, "how do Vivian or I put these devices under our feet so the authorities looking at surveillance tapes don't pick-up what happened? If we carry these into the room in a bag or something, wouldn't it be noticed? They'll obviously figure out where the gas came from, so all seven at the final table will be suspects, don't you think?"

"We thought of that," RJ told him. "What will happen is you will attach the device inside your pants, near your calf. Actually, correct that. We'll attach it. You'll need to be sure to wear loose fitting pants each day of the tournament, so that in reviewing any tapes, they don't see that D-day is the only day you'll have chosen to wear long pants. Anyway, we've fashioned a device that will allow you to release the cylinder to the floor without having to reach all the way down to your foot. You'll need to release soon after you sit down so that when they review the tapes and rewind from the gas explosion, they won't detect either you or Vivian making any unusual movements close to the time it goes off."

"So, we're lying there unconscious," Vivian said as though she was reading Paul's mind again. "Your guys have run off with the money and security is helping all the unconscious people. Meanwhile the video cameras are still running, and we have straps and strings, whatever, dangling out of our pant leg and *that* device under our foot?"

Paul found himself thanking whatever gods there be that this woman, reckless though she seemed to be, was too smart to be bulldozed by this man. Taking her out of this caper might not be as difficult as he had thought it might be.

"Well, not exactly," RJ told her, his bushy, dark eyebrows, furrowing. Clearly, he had detected the incredibility in her voice. "First the straps, as you called them, are really small pieces of thread that we will sew into your pant leg and like I said, you'll need to kick it to the center of the floor underneath the table."

RJ handed the two cylinders to Paul who passed one to Vivian. Paul weighed the light structure in his hand. He passed his fingers over the plunger, and the small eyelets, protruding from one end.

The technology for this device," RJ went on, "is superior, even when fully loaded with the gas and powder, it weighs almost the same as an empty beer can. It won't drag on your pants or show in any way. Furthermore, it won't take much pressure to pull the thread from outside your pants. There will be a small loop pulled through to the outside of your pants, like a snag. All you'll need to do is pull on one end of the thread and the quick release knot will allow the cylinder to fall down your leg. We'll also place a strap under the table that the authorities will think held the device. It will confuse them and make them think it had been planted before the tournament begins."

Paul was still holding a cylinder and trying to imagine it hanging from threads inside his pants. It was very light, but how the hell would this really work?

"Ok," Paul said, "how do we know when to exactly release this and set it off?"

"Good question," RJ said, reopening the briefcase and pulling out a small plastic bag. "The timing is critical for all of this. Here are some tiny, high tech receivers that will produce a discernable electric shook when activated. The entire team will have one taped under their watches."

RJ removed his watch and placed the thin little piece of green plastic on the under side.

Jesus Christ, thought Paul. What other little things does he have up his bony assed sleeve? It was like Mickey Mouse army games.

"They likely will not be discovered, but that's how we'll set everything in motion. Give me your watches now and I'll put them on. I'm not going to give you all the details of how we get out of the room, out of the hotel and clear the downtown area with thousands of cameras rolling. The only thing I'll tell you is that it maybe sixty to ninety days, or longer, before we can actually split up the money."

I can't believe he just said that, Paul thought. *I can't believe that I'm in a room with guys that would think I'm stupid enough to along with a scenario like that. That's crap. Vivian's got to know this as well as I do and if she doesn't, I'll sure as hell explain it to her. He ought to thank RJ for making this easy for him.*

"How can we trust that scenario?" Paul demanded. "We'll be questioned extensively by the police and perhaps even followed for days or weeks afterward. Everything will be searched, our bags, clothes, car, what have you. Crime scene folks will be testing our clothes trying to match cylinder gas residue, fingerprints and more. I just don't know, RJ."

Come on Vivian, read my mind now, Paul thought, *or wasn't this in your script?* Because much as he hated to admit it, there was always the off chance that she had conscripted him for this caper, that she had played poker on line for the express purpose of finding someone to seduce him into assisting in this enterprise – if you could call it that. Paul had not allowed himself to think of this possibility before, at least not consciously and he hated the way it made him feel. But all right, as long as he had come this far, why not go all the way and consider the possibility that she had helped RJ draft the mysterious third player, as well?

"RJ, we're not going to wait months to receive our split," Vivian was saying. "As Paul said, the authorities will be all over us. They're good at finding even the smallest shred of evidence. We take this huge risk with exploding gas bombs, and you expect us to trust that, at some future time, you somehow get us our cut? Come on, RJ."

"You guys have been watching way too much CSI on TV," he told her, lighting a Marlboro Red. "They're really not that good, but you will not have any evidence a crime lab will find anyway. They'll not take your clothes off. First, you'll receive your pants the night before the final day with the cylinder, all set to be released, assuming one of you is at the final table. You'll dress without touching it. We'll use a thread that matches the seams of your pants. If they happen to examine what you have on it will only look like some thread came lose from your seam. As far as the gas residue is concerned, everybody at the table will have remnants of powder and gas all over their clothes, particularly their pants, legs, and shoes. "

This had to be one of the most amateurish things he's ever heard, Paul told himself. Now's the time to cut to the chase on all this stuff.

"Let me ask you an important question," Vivian said, beating Paul to the punch. "Give us some confidence in all this by telling us you've done this before, using gas bombs, timing devices and other such things and grabbing cash or whatever in broad daylight."

"You're the fucking amateurs here," RJ said, sneering at Vivian. "I'll have you know that, although you brought this goddamn opportunity to our attention, it's what we do! These gas canisters are state-of-the-art, and cost a great deal. Don't question me!"

That little bastard, Paul thought. *He's thinking because he's got thugs to run in and grab the money and fancy gas bombs, his fucking ego makes him think he's impervious to better planning and ideas. Holy shit! The best he could do was stay calm, listen to the rest of all this nonsense, and get the hell out of here.*

"Okay, okay," Paul said. "So how do we contact each other and how will you pass Vivian or me the pants? You told me before you couldn't enter the casino yourself. Why is that?"

"Casinos in Vegas have introduced face recognition software," RJ said, in a more contained tone. "Since we're persons of interest, but with no convictions, we can't take the chance that their database has us in it. If we enter and we *are* in the base, an alarm goes off. Disguises don't work and they're more suspicious if you try to hide your identity. For months after the heist, they'll be searching their video files for anyone who might be interesting to them who entered the Four Queens within weeks prior to the tournament."

Paul looked down the table at RJ's bodyguards, if that's what they were. Jamey and Michael were staring at the ceiling and Alf was cleaning his fingernails.

"We have trusted people that will be our eyes and ears," RJ said handing Paul and Vivian's watches back to them, "people who will be there to scoop up the money. All you and Vivian need to do is send out some laundry items. I'll arrange to have them picked up and we'll rig your pants and deliver them back to your rooms the night before the final."

"RJ, you may as well know that Paul and I are in the same room," Vivian told him. "We're saving some expenses."

"Of course you're saving expenses," RJ said, raising his thick eyebrows. The way RJ looked at Vivian for an instant, Paul thought almost convinced him, Vivian wasn't in on this at all. "I'm sure you're sharing some other things too. I'll have to think about the consequences of you and Paul doing that. I wish you hadn't, but what is done is done."

Paul was surprised at how relieved he felt. If RJ had put Vivian up to this, he would have known all about how she had, presumably, talked Paul into it.

The meeting went on for another half hour or so as RJ went over the plan a couple more times and Vivian and Paul probed deeper into their roles and voiced some additional fears. RJ's answers to their questions continued to give Paul serious doubts about all this.

Okay, Paul thought, *I've given him all the time I need to convince him we're going to go through with this. How else for our safety, can I make him believe we're still very interested? Surely if we reject this now, we may not even get back to the Four Queens.* Paul, almost inadvertently, looked over at RJ's silent trio, scanning clothes for bulges of weapons. Yes, Jamey, leaning back, jacket opened slightly, exposing edge of a leather strap going over his shoulder. This guy was packing!

"Ok, RJ," Paul said, "now that we've heard the plan, and what our roles are to be in all this, forty-five or fifty percent is fair."

"Well, you don't know the whole plan," RJ said with that I could-kill-you-look, "and you have all you need to know, at any rate, I set the terms. It's thirty-five percent if one of you makes it to the final table and releases the gas. If the plan goes off without you, I'll still pay you ten thousand."

Hush money, Paul thought. *Time to get out of here.*

Before Paul could ask a final question and say he'd agree to the new split, Vivian, who had been leaning back in her chair, sat forward.

"Damn you, RJ," Vivian said, her voice rose a pitch and had none of her usual huskiness, "you were always a tightwad, flashing money around when it didn't matter. Paul and I will need to discuss this. Privately."

Big mistake, Paul thought. Didn't she realize that they need to get out of here now?

"No I don't think we need to discuss it," he said, "RJ's expenses being what they are, I think that thirty-five percent is okay."

Please don't say anything else Vivian, Paul thought. *Read my mind, now.* As if he willed it, Vivian merely turned to him and nodded. "I suppose you're right," she said and then almost inaudibly, "but it makes me mad."

Relieved, Paul asked a final question.

"I've been meaning to find out how people that get away with a large amount of cash actually go about spending it," Paul asked as earnestly as he could as they rose to go. "I mean I think the entire table will be suspects for a long time and spending large amounts of cash will certainly be a dead give-away, won't it?"

"You can pay cash for groceries, dinner out, and some furniture occasionally," RJ told him as he smoothed his black suit jacket and ran a hand through his greasy, curly hair. "The money will last you a very long time that way. Or we can help. We have ways of converting cash to harmless accounts, as you might expect." He gave a knowing glance at Vivian. "We have friends in the banking business."

The comment made Paul wonder if Vivian was telling the truth about Sara being gone from the laundering business.

"How will we stay in touch?" Paul asked as they were leaving the conference room.

"Yes, RJ, how do we stay in touch?" Vivian reiterated.

Paul was ready to swear now that she and RJ were not in cahoots. There was the kind of unspoken tension between them that never would have existed had they been conspirators in this.

RJ explained about his inside contacts being available at his beckon call and assured them that if needed he had his ways to contact them. They also agreed to another meeting at the same place at eleven in the evening, day after tomorrow.

As they all walked out together, they talked about how cool it was this time of night and the unusual wet winter, making it sound more like the end to a legitimate business meeting rather than the conclusion of a planning session for a two million dollar heist.

As he and Vivian drove off through the bright Las Vegas night, Paul was convinced that RJ was incompetent. Can't show his face in the casino. Exploding cylinders. Threads in pant legs. Money not split for months, if at all. Stupid watch gadget. If this is what a caper is, Paul thought, I'm glad to be done with it. But then, RJ maybe incompetent, but he could be *dangerous* and he needed to find out Vivian's real motive.

CHAPTER 15

PAUL WOKE WITH a start at four-thirty the next morning, not sure, what woke him.

He sensed the warm body of Vivian, inches from him. They had fallen asleep entwined together, their arms, legs and hands inseparable. Going over all the muddy details of the plan, he tried to figure out his next move. Hopefully, with Vivian's help, they could extricate themselves from this nonsensical plot and just concentrate on playing excellent poker and making love.

Paul slowly moved his hand down Vivian's body and rested it gently on her soft hair. He played with the hair and soft skin just at the space between her leg and where her hair starts. She stirred a bit and he stopped to see if she would wake.

Vivian remained motionless. His tongue and lips jealous of his fingers so close to her delectable cleft, he couldn't decide which to use. Vivian's legs parted slightly as he moved to her folds and felt the warm, moist soft skin. She moved again and moved her hips toward his hand. His fingers stopped moving, but he could feel the warmth and moisture emanating from her.

His mouth closer to her breasts, he gently nibbled on her. Inserting his fingers into the folds of the most wonderful, tight, hot place that he had known for some time, he could feel heft returning to him as he explored her breasts with his mouth and moved his fingers deeper. More slow hip movements and shallower breathing told him that he was bringing her out of her deep sleep. Her legs parted a little more as his finger slowly circled around in her opening and he continued to suck and nibble on her breast.

He smelled and savored the remnants of her perfume and bath scents, Vivian groaned slightly as he tasted her between her legs. Paul began to build in size as their pleasurable moans filled the room, her body stirred in response. As he kissed her body and breasts, he was at full mast. Although wanting to fill her with his hard shaft, he leisurely kissed and nibbled her breasts, neck, ears, and shoulders. Vivian's groans grew louder as he continued to kiss and fondle her. Holding back just outside of her, his mouth continued to devour her breasts. Concentrating on her neck and ears, his cock brushed the wet hair between her legs.

Reaching down to grab his manhood, Vivian seemed anxious to start the insertion process.

"Not yet," he whispered, moving out of her reach.

Kissing again, their tongues moved and danced. Her legs still parted, he knelt between them, kissing her neck, then her lips, moving around to her ears again and then on to her luscious breasts for a return visit. He wanted her to scream her desires to him and not hold back. As she whispered, "I want you, Paul, please – I'm aching to feel you inside of me," he continued to kiss her and hold himself just outside of her body. He, too, was overcome with desire, but he still didn't let on. More time on her breasts and then gently biting her nipples. God, he wanted to enter her.

"Oh Paul, now!" Vivian uttered, as if reading his mind, again. "I want you inside of me."

Both moaned in pleasure as Paul drove to the hilt. He knew now that, in spite of the eagerness he felt now, the previous violent ejaculation of five hours earlier might have taken a bit out of him, which meant that he would be able to thrust deep inside her for a long while.

When the alarm buzzed, Paul raised his head and squinted at the clock. "Oh God Paul," Vivian said, "was I dreaming last night or did we make fantastic love again?"

"No dream, my dear," Paul said as he caressed her cheek. "Actually it was early this morning. It was fantastic, wasn't it?"

After showering together while waiting for room service, Paul emerged from the bathroom first, put on his short terry cloth robe, and turned on the TV. He had a feeling he was forgetting something as he placed the poker chips left out from the night before back into the container. And then he remembered. Maureen! Shit, he thought, he should call her soon.

Over breakfast, they talked about RJ's plan. First Paul, and then Vivian tried to poke holes in it, but for now at least, they avoided articulating the obvious decision.

"I don't know about you," Vivian finally said. "But I'm feeling guilty about bringing you into this mess. I had no idea that RJ would have thought up such a risky plan. Gas canisters indeed. How are you feeling about actually participating in it?"

"Oh, Vivian," Paul said, breathing a sigh of relief. "I'm so happy to hear you say that. That was really the decision I came to last night as I heard the absurd plan unfold. You know him better than I. But I think we need to be very careful about how we tell him we're not going to play. If he decides to go ahead with his so-called plan B player, he won't want us in the know. And we know a lot already. We're are too dangerous to him, particularly if we're questioned, or become suspects as well. I don't think he can afford to think we might talk."

"You're not suggesting," Vivian said, her voice low and serious. "That he'd have us killed, are you?"

"Yes, I am," Paul said. "Think about it for a minute. RJ may have not come up with a plan that suits us, but he is walking around a free man, which would indicate at least to me, that he's been a careful crook. I believe he's quite capable of removing any risks or obstacles in any manner that suits him, including murder."

"You don't think," Vivian said, eyes widening. "that if we just told him we weren't going to go along with him and promised to keep quiet, he'd let us be? I never saw a violent side to him."

"I don't trust him, at all," said Paul. "You didn't see him at work did you? I bet he's never told you the truth about what he really does or has done in the past. Money laundering, swindles, whatever he told you he did, I guarantee that's only a fraction of the crimes he's really committed. I definitely don't want to chance him being benevolent. Besides, that Jamey character was definitely carrying a gun. I wouldn't be surprised if all of them were."

Apparently deep in thought, Vivian began to pace around the room.

"Come to think of it," she finally said, "Sara did mention to me a couple of times that these guys could be dangerous, when she said she was going to tell them she wanted out of the laundering business. What an idiot I've been, Paul. Can you ever forgive me?"

"Here's what I think we should do," Paul said. "We have all day today and tomorrow before we have to meet him again. So let's play our asses off and when we get the chance, talk about how we get ourselves out of this mess. I've got a few ideas, but I need to let them percolate for a while."

"Yes, I like that approach," Vivian said, coming over to embrace him. "I'll think on it too."

"We'll just have to just see how this plays out." Paul said finally, "If worse comes to worse, we can always not step on the plunger and tell him it didn't work! Now let's get dressed and play some poker."

Unlike the WSOP where there were well over four thousand contestants and many separate rounds, this smaller tournament started and finished in the same room. Because they already had their entry forms and receipts, Paul and Vivian pushed their way through the throng of registrants. One table was marked; "Satellite Winners and Paid Entrants." The other table's sign displayed, "Registrants and Qualifiers." Paul recognized many of the players lined up at the sign-in tables where the final fee had to be paid. As he and Vivian were waiting for the tournament clerk to finish providing their forms, seat assignment and chips, Paul noticed several security guards standing about, mostly engaged in idle chat as well as several TV camera operators wielding ESPN logos on their cameras, taking shots of the crowd. They seemed to be following a particular player, Paul saw it was Chris Moneymaker, one of several favored to win. It was still about thirty minutes before they would get under way.

Paul's only chance to be alone was when, just before he and Vivian entered the tournament room, he went to the restroom where he dialed Maureen's work number, hoping to get her voice mail. Since it was nearly noon, his chances were good that Maureen would be tied up for lunch. He was in luck. When her VM kicked in, Paul left a short, apologetic message, telling her that the next time he would have a chance to call it would probably be too late at night. It wasn't a great excuse, he knew, but it was enough to ease his guilt for another twenty-four hours or so.

As he and Vivian made their way into the room, after kissing and wishing each other luck, they made their way to their assigned tables, she at table sixteen and he at twenty. The sea of poker tables, green felt, and lights made his pulse quicken. This is why he's was here, Paul thought as he anxiously stacked his chips, waiting for the dealer and other players to appear. The room, surrounded by a low set of bleachers behind felt ropes, had a warm feeling. Two exit doors at the far end, away from the entrance, had him wondering about RJ's get-a-way. Glancing at the ceiling Paul counted six round surveillance domes and about six or seven cameras without the domes, pinned to the cross members of the dropped ceiling, pointing at odd angles. One of them perched, as it was above his table, looked down at him, menacingly. .

The room continued to fill with players, fanning out to look for their tables. Paul saw some formidable contenders such as Barry Greenstein, Chris Lindenmayer, Chris 'Jesus' Ferguson, checking their slips and finding their tables, but none of them joined him at table twenty

His dealer was a young man in his late twenties, dressed in a purple smock with the Four Queens in gold on his left chest. As player after player took their place at the table, he checked names and receipts.

Paul heard all the names as the dealer went through his ID checks, and then forgot them instantly. The other players all looked redoubtable, including a young man in his early twenties wearing a UNLV –"Go Rebels" tee shirt. Neither he nor the others looked like they would know RJ, but then, Paul thought neither did he or Vivian. There were no women at his table, but he knew there were almost a dozen or so female entrants. Paul turned his attention to the tournament information sheet:

EACH LEVEL WILL LAST ONE HOUR,
WITH A 20-MINUTE BREAK AFTER
EVERY OTHER LEVEL. A ONE-HOUR
DINNER BREAK AFTER LEVEL 5.

L E V E L	ANTE	B L I N D S
1ST	-	$100-$200
2ND	-	$100-$200
3RD	-	$100-$200
4TH	-	$200-$400
5TH	$50	$400-$800
6TH	$100	$400-$800
7TH	$125	$400-$800

MINIMUM BET - $500

AT THE END OF ROUND SEVEN,
TOURNAMENT OFFICIAL WILL DECIDE
THE ANTE AND BLINDS FOR ROUND
EIGHT, BASED ON PLAYERS REMAINING.
ALL PLAY WILL END BY 10:00 PM THE
FIRST THREE DAYS. DAY FOUR WILL
ONLY END WHEN THE SEVEN PLAYERS
REMAIN.

FINAL DAY – MAY 5, PLAY WILL
COMMENCE AT NOON AND CONTINUE
UNTIL THERE IS ONE WINNER.

This tournament, Paul knew, would be a fast one. If a player hit a bad streak, he could depart very early with some large calls on an "all-in." Even the best of them could lose their $10 thousand in chips in short order if they were not careful. The Four Queens would reset the levels and timing at each daily session depending on the number of players and tables left in the tournament. Tournament officials had figured a way for the last table to start at noon on May 5th, for a grand finale and Cinco de Mayo celebration. Little did they know the 5th of May this year could go down in Las Vegas history for some other reason!

When the dealer, with a flourish, dealt the first hand, Paul took a deep breath, held it, and picked up his cards. Three and five off suited. Fold. He had a chance to calm his nerves as the table played without him on the first hand. Next hand he would be at the big blind.

After a complete circle of the table, Paul took a little comfort that he had won a couple of small pots, and folded with a pair of tens after the flop of two Q's and an ace. The young UNLV man won the biggest pot so far, but Paul still had more chips than when he started, and Paul was on the big blind when he received a pair of K's. A man wearing a Hawaiian shirt kicked up the big blind up by $500. Everybody else folded. Paul called, and moved in his $700. The flop was K, six, nine. Paul pushed in two $500 chips. "Raise." Hawaiian Shirt called and re-raised $1500. Paul was sure he had him unless the man was looking for a straight, holding a seven, eight. He could have trip sixes or nines. What was this guy thinking? Paul called.

The turn helped neither of them, a trey. Paul pushed in a $1000 chip, and stared at Hawaiian Shirt. Hawaiian Shirt stared back. He folded and Paul pulled in the modest pot.

Toward the end of level two, Paul received a diamond suited A, K. The blinds were still a modest, $200/400. He was in last position after the deal and watched the raises from each player advance around the table to him. He had to put in $2200 to call, but decided to slow-play his ace and K, so Paul did not raise, but just called instead. The pot was over $15,000.

The flop was a J of diamonds, ten of hearts, ace of clubs. Paul looked around the table. Paul needed a Q for a straight and he was sure of the action earlier someone might have trip J's or aces. Since Paul already had an ace in the pocket, the odds were slim. He tried to remember the odds from his book table. Corduroy Shirt, a man in his forties, checked. Two more folds and Hawaiian Shirt and UNLV also checked. The man to his right, wearing a very strong dose of Old Spice, checked. A cameraman came by and took shots of all the players, probably for later use during the broadcast. Paul hoped this hand would provide good action for the ESPN audience.

So fourteen cards out, one buried and three on the flop. It was likely that, of the remaining thirty-four, he would get face card or a ten on the turn or the river. Based on the first round of betting, however, of the fourteen cards out, perhaps ten or twelve of them were already at that value. "All in," Paul announced, pushing in all of his chips to convey the impression that he had ace, top high straight. Good time to bluff, thought Paul. The six other players seemed to suck in their breaths simultaneously. Then, just as he hoped, all of them folded.

While Paul raked in his chips, the others became animated for the first time.

"You're not going to show your pocket?"

"How about I pay you $10 to look at your cards?"

Corduroy Shirt slammed down his cards. "Shit," he said. "I'm throwing in trip tens!" Paul quietly stacked his chips and remained silent. He wanted the rest of the tournament players to hear about this.

After Paul folded three times in succession, once again with a pair of tens, but he was setting the stage for later, a chime sounded indicating a twenty-minute break. Stretching, Paul stood up, and went to find Vivian.

As he made his way though the crowd he met Vivian, wearing such a broad smile there was no need to ask how she'd done.

Sitting at a couple of empty slot machines in the casino, they lit up and compared games. Both had raked in large pots. Like Paul's, Vivian's table was still intact, but she had seen several players leaving from tables near her.

Play resumed though the next two levels until shortly after level four started, Paul had folded along with everybody but UNLV Shirt, and Old Spice. Old Spice, looked at the flop of a pair of J's and ten. Paul was sure Old Spice had at least trip J's. When UNLV asked the dealer to count the chips, he announced he was all-in. His wager was $9,000. After UNLV counted out his $9,000, he had about $200. left in front of him which would mean the end of him if he lost the next hand.

The players turned over their cards and waited for the turn and river. Old Spice did indeed have a pair of J's. UNLV had a pair of tens. The turn revealed a seven, which meant no help for either of them, leaving Old Spice in the driver's seat. Incredibly, the river was a ten. UNLV, whom Paul now knew as Tim, jumped up, circled around with his hands in the air celebrating, much to the general interest of other players. Old Spice picked up his water bottle and picture of his wife, shook hands with Tim, wished the table good luck, and departed with his head hanging low.

Paul counted his chips and discovered that he had $24,500, while UNLV would have $30,000 and the chip lead for now. Paul sized the other player's chips and decided he was in second place, which meant he could play conservatively, if necessary, for the next three rounds and hang on to see what the officials had in store for level eight tonight.

That night, he and Vivian had a pizza for dinner at the small Pizzeria tucked away just above the casino, delighted that they were both doing so well.

"I won an incredible pot," Vivian said proudly. "I was sitting on a club suited ten, jack, and a man wearing a tank top, raised the big blind by $2000. I called, naturally, and reraised him $2000. The guy was twitching all over the place, and I was sure I had picked up his tell earlier. I was almost positive his pocket didn't contain a pair, and even if it had, I was feeling good about this hand."

Vivian was her old self now, full of excitement and confidence in her skill talking about poker. Paul was happy in her exuberance and had renewed confidence that poker and him, was all the excitement she needed in her life.

"Anyway," she went on. "Everybody else folded so it was he and I, staring at each other. He twitched some more and called my reraise. The flop contained three small clubs, so I'm sitting on a flush. I knew then, that even if he had a high pair, he'd have to turn a boat to beat me. I didn't even bother to check, I just bet ten grand. Unbelievably, he called me, but didn't reraise, so I knew he had to have only a pair. I was right, as the turn and the river had nothing. It was a big pot."

"Great playing, Vivian," Paul told her, taking her arm.

When Paul asked if she noticed anybody that might be RJ's other inside man. Vivian said *him*. Why, she asked, did he think it had to be a *man*?

"I was using man as in mankind." Paul told her. "Beside I think RJ said *man*."

"Sure you were." Vivian replied, giving Paul that wry smile, he recognized as trying for female superiority.

Level's six and seven passed, with Paul gaining on UNLV, while Corduroy, Hawaiian Shirt and the three other unremarkable players continued their losing streak. During the break as the officials took a player and chip count, Paul and Vivian dragged on cigarettes and speculated about what the ante and blinds would be for the remaining hour of play.

"I think they'd like the tournament to be down to a hundred players or so for tomorrow so they can add room for more audience by removing some tables," Paul told her. "Just eyeballing the empty seats, I'd say there were over a hundred players left."

"How many players need to be eliminated each day so there are only seven of us left on May 5?" Vivian asked.

"That's the beauty of the way they're working this." Paul told her. "They can wait until day four to decide how severe to make the antes and blinds. They also have the option to extend the play on days three and four if there aren't enough players losing."

"So maybe we can get to bed at a decent time tonight," Vivian observed, grinning. "But, remember that we have to meet RJ tomorrow night. That could be a big problem, you know. If the play gets extended we could be late, assuming we're both still in."

"RJ will know if we are playing past ten," Paul said. "I guarantee it. He seems to have eyes and resources everywhere, I also guarantee we'll both be in it because we're both playing so well. Don't start

173

losing your confidence on me, Vivian. By the way, when you fold a hand take a moment to think about D-day and everything that could go wrong because we'll have to convince the police that we knew nothing about it. We need to make sure we ask RJ all the right questions tomorrow night, making him think we're still in his crazy plot until we figure out how to extricate ourselves. We will need to be ready for a tough several days coming up. This will be the biggest thing to hit Vegas in sometime and it will be all over the news for weeks. If it wasn't for that veiled threat of his and our belief he could be very dangerous, I have half a mind to call the cops right now."

On their way back to the tournament room, Paul thought of all the possible ways to end this crazy situation. But none made sense. He had to think, damn it. Think. The last thing he wanted was that dangerous son of a bitch, RJ, deciding that he had a good reason to eliminate both him and Vivian in more ways than one.

CHAPTER 16

WHEN THEY RETURNED to the poker room, the officials had posted a new sign.

Level 8 – Ante - $500. Blinds - $1000/$2000.
MINIMUM BET 1000

Play will end at 10:30 PM

Beside the sign was a computer printout of all the players with about two dozen names crossed out.

"See how aggressive they're making this. They need to get it down under a hundred tonight." Paul said. "My guess is there are still about hundred and twenty or so of us left."

Later, the hotel room door locked securely behind them they embraced passionately.

"I've been giving this thing some thought," Vivian said, standing back and looking deeply into Paul's eyes. "But I want to apologize again for getting you mixed up in all this."

"No need to apologize, please," Paul said, "I'm just so glad we're now on the same wavelength. I've been thinking about it too. What'd you come up with?"

"Well," Vivian began. "I'm not sure what to do at the final table on D-day, but I think it's important we find out who RJ's other man is, and I don't know how to find out short of just asking him."

"That's right," Paul said. "I was thinking the same thing. "The safest way for us to get out of this, it seems to me, is to let RJ believe we're going to carry out his crazy plan. We need to think about a way, when we're at the final table," Paul said exuding confidence, "to make it look like something just didn't go right."

"Yes, yes," Vivian said. "That's more or less what I was thinking. You don't think all three of us would be required to have those silly cylinders, do you?"

"I'm not sure what he's thinking," Paul said, "But I'm assuming, based on his original comments, that only one of us needs the canister even though we'll all probably have our pants modified to carry that stupid canister. We'll just have to wait until tomorrow night and see what he says or wants us to do."

They were interrupted by a knock on the door. It was a bellman wearing the hotel's distinctive blue uniform, who said he was there to pick up some laundry.

Well, damn, Paul thought after the bellman left carrying whatever Vivian had been able to put her hands on quickly, that bastard does have resources. He and she were in more danger than he had thought and what the hell was he going to do about it?"

Their lovemaking that night was intense while, at the same time, relieving some of the stress they had both been under. The hard day of poker and thinking about how they could get out of RJ's caper had drained them. Vivian never did get to put on a 'flimsy thing.' They sprawled together on the big bed and fell sound asleep.

They awoke almost at the same time. Paul was feeling very comfortable with Vivian now, but somehow Maureen kept popping into his head. He would have to call her again, he knew sometime soon. And what was he going to tell her? Because he knew for certain now that she was not the way he wanted to go.

As soon after Vivian disappeared into the bathroom, Paul put on a pair of shorts and a tee shirt, grabbed his cell phone and card key, and went down the hall to vending. When he passed a hotel house cleaner, his immediate thought was she could be an RJ spy. Paranoia really set in as he waited for the maid to enter a room. Ducking into the alcove, he punched in Maureen's number.

Walking down the hallway with a bucket of ice, and a bad case of the guilts. Paul mulled over his conversation with Maureen. She had been disappointed, as he had assumed she would, about his lack of calls and progress reports. He and Vivian seemed to be in harmony now, but he still wasn't a hundred percent sure of Vivian's motives in all this. Was Vivian just saying the right things? Was RJ doing all this to try to win her back, knowing she had a larcenous side? He felt terrible about having to make these dutiful and almost demanding calls to Maureen. But, in spite of her clinging and demanding ways, Maureen certainly represented a safety he wasn't currently feeling with Vivian. His focus for now was winning and knocking RJ and whom ever his accomplice was out of the picture.

Paul and Vivian found the new Level scheme pulled back a bit from last night's final round.

EACH LEVEL WILL LAST ONE HOUR, WITH A 20-MINUTE BREAK AFTER EVERY OTHER LEVEL. A ONE-HOUR DINNER BREAK AFTER LEVEL 5.

ALL $50 CHIPS WILL BE EXCHANGED FOR HIGHER DENOMINATIONS.

L E V E L	ANTE	B L I N D S
1ST	$500	$800-$1600
2ND	$500	$800-$1600
3RD	$500	$800-$1600
4TH	$500	$800-$1600
5TH	$1000	$1600-$3200
6TH	TBD	TBD
7TH	TBD	TBD

MINIMUM BET - $1000

AT THE END OF LEVEL FIVE, TOURNAMENT OFFICIALS WILL DECIDE THE ANTE AND BLINDS FOR THE REMAINING ROUNDS BASED ON PLAYERS REMAINING. ALL PLAY WILL END BY 10:00 PM.

Vivian and Paul registered, that the chip count was what they turned in the night before and drew table numbers for the days' play. Vivian drew table six and Paul nine. "That's a good sign," Vivian whispered as they wended their way into the room. "My favorite numbers."

Paul noticed that there had been some changes. Table one had been moved a bit closer to the security ropes and more rows of bleacher type seats added, as well as additional lights that presumably would allow ESPN to tape more of the action, making the room look like more a TV set. Paul saw that several players had beaten him to the table today. Assigned seat five, he placed his water bottle, and chips in front of him and sat down and introduced himself to Chau Giang, Steve Zolotow, and the first female to face him, Jennifer Harman a middle-aged brunette dressed in a navy blue sweatshirt with gold "Four Queens" in sequins across her full chest. All of them seemed to be doing pretty well, but Paul making a quick estimate of the chips stacked in front of each, decided that of the four of them, Paul had the chip lead.

At hand three, Paul folded for the third time and everyone else passed except Jennifer who made it $15,000 to go from the button, a good positional raise.

"Aren't you a little curious?" she asked.

Chau Giang, a heavy hitter, winning lots of tournaments as Paul remembered from magazine articles, stared at her and finally said, "All-in." Whereupon the table folded except for Jennifer, who asked of no one in particular, "What do I do now?" before finally calling, pushing in her required amount of chips.

Jennifer turned over her A-Q, and Giang turned over pocket eights. Paul watched intently as the dealer spilled out a six, three, six, followed by a three, and a five. Goodbye Jennifer. After only three hands, the only female Paul had faced so far was gone. Paul noticed Giang smirking and thought he would get him soon!

By the end of level two, another player left with a losing "All-in" to the hard-hitting Zolotow. At one point, he heard the small crowd that had gathered on the bleachers, erupt into applause and oohhhs, sounding much as they would if a golf pro had missed a close putt and glancing up to see Chris Moneymaker leaving table one. It would be interesting to see the list and determine the 'power players' that remained.

When the break finally came, Vivian and Paul found seats at a couple of video poker machines and told one another about the last few hours of play, play that had garnered, almost $55,000 in chips. Even at that, with the next levels of ante and blinds, that amount of money could be eaten up in a hurry.

"It finally happens," Someone on the other sided of the poker machines was saying excitedly. "I'm dealt ace, ten of hearts in a middle position. Bob is big blind. I call the blind. When action gets to him, he raises $15 thousand. Now ace ten of hearts is not the best starting hand, but I know he is loose and I will act last on all subsequent rounds so I call."

A cocktail server asked if they wanted drinks interrupting their eavesdropping and Paul shook his head. Paul wanted to find out who was talking on the other side as it could be good information for them to use later on. He could not see who might have been talking, and sat down. "I think they are gone."

"Too bad," Vivian said. "Man, this is certainly exciting. Everybody is so wired. Poker players are so great to listen too. I can't get enough of this action!"

"Notice anything we should take to the meeting with RJ tonight?" Paul said, changing the subject. "Doors, guards, players, anything to make him think we're still going to do this?"

"No, I haven't. Actually, I've been so focused on playing, I didn't give it a thought." Vivian confessed. "And frankly, just not thinking of RJ was a relief. I can't imagine what got into me to think it would be a good idea. It's exciting enough just to be here with you."

They agreed to be more observant and if they made it through the day, the odds would be considerably higher that they would be at same table very soon.

"There's an ESPN photographer that seems to be taking a lot of shots of me," Vivian said. "Sometimes he makes me lose my concentration. I'd really be nervous at table number one, with pocket cards being broadcast and close-ups all the time."

"You're the most beautiful woman here," Paul told her. "A few shots of your face alone will increase their ratings. I'm so proud to know you. Say, I think we can get in and out of Hugo's in an hour. Let me make reservations for dinner after level five so that we can celebrate our playing so far. Wait here. I'll be right back."

Paul and Vivian increased their chip counts during the next two levels before meeting in the doorway for the dinner break. And then, at Hugo's that evening, Paul told the waiter they were in the tournament and needed to be out of there in an hour. Paul and Vivian ordered ice teas, intent on keeping their heads clear. Paul told himself that he would have a martini, if he made through the rest of the day's levels, and had time. And he would certainly have one before the meeting with RJ.

"I just love this place," Vivian told him. She was looking especially beautiful today in a form fitting yellow silk blouse, with buttons running up to her neck. Being the consummate professional poker player that she was, the excitement of the play had brought a flush to her cheeks that made her look even more amazing, and Paul knew that tonight would be just as special as their first dinner together had been.

"I love this place, too," Paul said, holding her hand. "I can't wait to be touching your skin again."

"Me too," Vivian purred, "But let's talk poker. How did you do? I took out two players, including Chris Lindenmayer who has been getting a lot of press lately."

Paul grinned, "The way we are going, one of us just may, repeat may, just make it to the final table on Thursday."

And then, as the waiter placed their entrees in front of them, a very large man, weighing at least two-hundred and seventy pounds, and almost as tall as Paul, approached their table. "Hi," he said. "Please forgive the interruption, but is your name Paul Langley?"

Who is this guy interrupting our dinner, Paul thought. *If I don't stand up, maybe he'll go away.*

"My name is Greg Raymer and I heard you were playing very well," he said in a staccato voice. "And you must be Vivian Davis. I wanted to meet you both and wish you the best. It's not often that those of us in the regular poker circles are invaded by a couple of newbie's that do so well through the first several days. We might be playing each other tomorrow and just wanted to meet you both. Please don't let me take you from your dinners. Just one other thing, are you guys playing in the "WSOP" at the Rio next month?"

"Nope," said Paul. "We have day jobs, and at least speaking for me, I couldn't get that kind of time off. Maybe next year."

"Well, you should consider it," Greg told them. "You both play excellently from what I have heard. Enjoy the rest of your meal."

As soon as he left, Paul and Vivian looked at each other and laughed. "How about that," said Paul, "Seems we have been doing fabulously indeed."

"That is a big guy," Vivian said as she started to cut into her steak. "I can see someone like him making things a little difficult for those would-be robbers at the Bellagio last year."

Paul lit their after dinner cigarettes with ten minutes to spare to the start of the next level.

"I did have a chance to look under a poker table," he said in a low voice. "And I am still worried about one of us being a suspect even if we don't do anything. They'll figure out that the cylinder had to be planted and discharged by one of the finalists. We need to get our stories straight about where we have been, that sort of thing. For instance, the valet could tell that we left the hotel the night before the tournament and they may ask where we went. Since we didn't go to a club or another casino, we won't have an alibi. And we'll have no alibi again tonight. Let's make sure we cover that with RJ when we see him."

When they returned to the tournament room, the officials obviously thought play was proceeding according to schedule, as the remaining levels for the night did not have any major changes. They only increased the ante and added a note about tomorrow's play:

L E V E L	ANTE	B L I N D S
6 & 7	$2000	$1600-$3200
7TH	TBD	TBD

MINIMUM BET $4000

PLEASE NOTE THAT TOMORROW'S (MAY
4) PLAY WILL BEGIN AS USUAL AT NOON
AND LEVEL ANTES, MINIMUM BETS,
AND BLINDS – WILL BE DETERMINED
AFTER ANALYSIS OF REMAINING

PLAYERS AND CHIP COUNTS. All $100 AND $500 DENOMINATION CHIPS WILL BE REMOVED/EXCHANGED.

ALL PLAY WILL END WHEN THE FINAL SEVEN PLAYERS ARE DETERMINED. PLEASE NOTE THIS MAY BE EARLY OR VERY LATE. PLAY ON 'CINCO DE MAYO' WILL COMMENCE AT NOON.

Paul continued to play well for the next two hours and increased his chip count considerably. He had come to realize that Vivian was a superb player and likely was doing well also. Paul noted that although about a dozen players left the room before the bell chimed an end to round seven, the audience in the bleacher seats had grown considerably as had the activity of the ESPN camera operators as they moved about the room, capturing images of the remaining players.

At one point Paul wished he had drawn table one, in order to become accustomed to the lights and pocket cameras hidden in the tables' edge. Perhaps tomorrow, he thought. Then again, if he and Vivian continued at separate tables, and only played against each other on the final day, they would have to decide who would interfere with RJ's plan. Then it occurred to him, that if only one of them made it to the final table, assuming RJ provided two of them, they would have to dispose of the extra cylinder sometime before the final event started. Easy to do, he thought, or otherwise, it would be discovered if the police searched their room. Paul blanched at the thought. This was something RJ would have to clean up when they meet tonight. He wondered what else he had not thought of.

Paul had not yet taken care of Chau Giang, his smirking opponent, when he received a pair of aces. *Now was clearly the time*, Paul thought as he raised the big blind to $10,000., from his late position. Giang called while everyone else folded apparently prepared to watch Paul and Giang duke it out. When the flop turned out to be an unsuited ace, ten, K, Paul was sure he had him even though he knew that Giang may have a pair of cowboys and could have flopped a set, knowing that the ace would give Giang pause for a moment and would probably check. He did. Paul looked at Giang for a sign but he only continued to smirk across the green felt. Paul decided to slow raise with a modest bet of $5,000. Perhaps Giang would take that as a sign of weakness or assume he was slowing playing from power. Paul hoped he would think the latter.

Giang called and did not re-raise. The turn dropped a ten. Now this was getting very interesting. Paul decided that Giang did in fact have a pair of K's. If Giang had a pair of tens as well, Paul was finished. On the other hand, they could both have a full boat. Paul waited for what seemed like an eternity for Giang to do something. "Could be a coin flip." He heard Giang mutter. Paul was hoping his slow raise had given Giang a hint that he didn't have a pair of aces, when Giang announced, "All-in." A textbook move, thought Paul

After sorting furiously through his memorized list of probabilities based on how Giang had played on previous hands, Paul decided, that he didn't have pocket tens. Giang was 'steaming,' playing all out aggressively. "Call," Paul said in a low voice, causing the other players to move to their elbows as the dealer counted out their chips. An ESPN cameraman appeared and hovered over the table, recording the action.

It was a powerful moment. If Paul lost, he would not be completely out, but if he won, Giang would be gone and Paul would have the chip lead at the table. Paul shuffled his remaining chips as he waited for the dealer to make the pot right, and then Paul and Giang revealed their cards. Giang did, indeed, have a pair of K's, but his expression didn't change when Paul revealed his aces. Only a king on the river could save Giang now. The player wearing Boston Red Sox gear was smiling broadly at Paul, which told him that the guy had a king before he folded. They waited for the river; Paul now knew it could not be a king. The dealer dropped the final card, it's a harmless five. Bye, bye Giang.

Play ended almost precisely at ten, and even though they were anxious about the meeting and full of ideas on how to deal with RJ, it took Vivian and Paul more time than they wanted to turn in their chips, sign paperwork, and get out of the poker room.

"Damn, Vivian," Paul said in the elevator. "I was hoping to have more time to discuss our strategy for the meeting.

"You know," Vivian said. "I've been thinking about that too, but you know, we're two very smart people and I think we'll think of something as the meeting unfolds. At our meeting with him, the other night, I thought we were on the same wavelength most of the time. The point is that we have to get out of this without putting either on of us in danger."

"I was going to tell you the same thing," Paul said as they exited the elevator. "Sometimes you did seem to read my mind. Look, I agree. The important thing is to get out of this with our skins still wrapped around our bodies. We must find out who the other player is. If we're going to stop this stupid plan, I think it's important we know who we're playing against. We're playing so well, I think we'll just win the money."

When they reached their room, they saw that two envelopes, each marked with the Four Queens logo, had been slid under the door.

They contained a questionnaire for each of them from the ESPN announcing crew, asking for their general backgrounds so they could fill in the audience as play progressed tomorrow, advancing to the final day.

"Shit, we have to fill these out and turn them in by ten tomorrow morning," mused Paul.

"All they want is the usual stuff; children, spouse, hobbies, previous poker tournaments," Vivian said reading her copy. "It won't take us long. Did you see this at the bottom? They want us in the media room at ten to shoot a short interview. I guess that's for use during the finals, if we're in it."

"The way we're playing, there's no doubt in my mind we will be there," Paul said.

"We are doing so well, aren't we?" she said, hugging him.

"Yes, and I suppose it will still give RJ some hope we'll be willing accomplices," Paul said trying not to imagine the worst-case scenario involving cement and a lot of water. "We should get going."

While he was waiting for Vivian to change her clothes, Paul made mental notes of all the questions and concerns he had for RJ. Vivian interrupted his serious thinking by appearing and looking lovely and particularly sexy in a green halter top, and a very short pleated white skirt that accented her long legs and white, cross-strapped sandals, her red hair still cascading about her shoulders.

But a single question stuck in the back of his mind. This woman had said all the right things, treated him beautifully, and seemed to be in accord with dumping RJ and his plan. He just wished he could remove the last of his doubts about her.

CHAPTER 17

ON THEIR WAY to the rendezvous, Vivian handed Paul a pair of silk panties.

"Does this mean what I think it means?" He asked, all of the thoughts of the meeting with RJ temporarily dashed from his mind.

"You'll just have to explore and find out for yourself." Vivian said coyly. Encouraged by her hand on his, he moved higher.

"Damn, you are an exciting woman!" he said, breathing harder and trying to concentrate on his driving. "I hope we don't crash."

"Oh, you're so close now, Paul. Don't stop." Vivian scooted down in the seat raising her white short skirt, as Paul found her neatly trimmed area.

Vivian placed her hand on Paul's engorging groin area as Paul's finger started to work just inside Vivian's tight opening. He moved his finger around in the wetness as Vivian massaged the length of his shaft, which was now moving down his leg. When they pulled to a stop light, a cab pulled up next to them, but Vivian apparently could have cared less about being seen. It was easy to believe that that her sex life thrived on danger.

"Okay. Okay." Paul gasped when the light finally turned green. "We have to stop. We're almost there."

"Damn Vivian, we're so done with our foreplay that you're in big trouble when we get back to the room." He sucked on his finger. "Mmmm, tastes so good!"

Speaking of tasting good, "I think I'll swallow you tonight." Vivian's voice had that husky quality that he loved.

"Oh Jeez. It will never go down now. Look at what you've done." He looked down at his lap. Even in the dim light from the dashboard lights, his manhood was quite evident.

"God! RJ should see that," Vivian said patting it. "He would have a jealous fit. And just so you know my studley man, RJ's not that good a lover either."

Paul pulled the BMW next to the black Cadillac at the rear of the office building. Time to get back to reality. "I guess they're already inside," he said, looking around nervously. "We are only a few minutes late."

Paul got out of the car, circled the car, and opened Vivian's door. When Paul helped Vivian out of the car, she flashed him, parting her legs as she swivel in the seat to get out. "God you are sexy," Paul breathed as he pulled her out of the car.

Finding the rear entrance unlocked, they proceeded down the hall and entered the conference room, hand holding, to find RJ and Alf seated at the end of the table. "Good evening," RJ said, standing. "I hear you both played brilliantly today."

Okay you son of a bitch, let's get on with this, Paul thought as he maneuvered himself between Vivian and RJ.

"Well, I have good news and bad news," RJ said when they were seated. "The good news is that our other man is still in the contest."

"See," Paul said in a low voice, "I told you it was a man."

"I can guess that Vivian's is giving you crap about women and all that." RJ said. Tonight he was wearing an expensive floral designed silk shirt with Chino trousers along with the same menacing look.

"Oh, I don't need to give him nearly as bad a time as I did you," Vivian assured him, smiling. "Paul knows how to treat women in today's world."

What's with that friendly banter, thought Paul. Damn, just when he was thinking Vivian couldn't be collaborating with RJ, doubt springs forward again.

"Okay, that's enough," RJ said, scowling. "Now the bad news. We've been doing some analysis of how the feds or cops will investigate the crime. As I told you the other night, Vivian, I wish you hadn't decided to stay in Paul's hotel room. As a result of that bit of carelessness, we're going to use our other man. I want you both out of the tournament."

"What," exclaimed Paul and Vivian simultaneously.

RJ raised his hand. "We don't like the risks," he said.

"But, RJ, you knew we were going to be together when we first spoke about this," Vivian interrupted him. "Why change your mind now?"

"I'm not changing my mind now!" RJ looked furious. "And listen up. I don't want any crap from either of you on this. My mind's made up and if either of you is considering telling anybody about this, there'll be very serious consequences." He pointed his bony finger at

Vivian, "And I mean *consequences!* The only reason I'm keeping you in the mix now is because I need you out of the running for final play and help make sure our other man makes it to the finals."

"Oh, RJ that's not right." Vivian said angrily.

Let it be, Vivian. I can see if you're with him or me, thought Paul as what RJ had just said sunk in. This was actually a fortunate turn of events. They could just win it all and RJ could go fuck himself. The only thing they needed to do now was to find out who the other player was. Paul continued to think furiously. Officially expelled from the risky plan, he could now concentrate on winning and stopping RJ from pulling off this stupid heist. On the other hand, what did serious consequences mean?

Vivian would not let up, "Damn you, RJ," she exclaimed. "I cannot believe this. You expect us to lose tomorrow so that we will not be at the final table and help your unidentified man make it. Then you're going to deny us our share because you're concerned about Paul and I being together."

Of all of Vivian's qualities, thought Paul, she was also one hell of an actress. Was she acting for me, to make sure RJ thought we were unhappy about being told to leave it, or was she acting for RJ to make me believe she wasn't still conspiring with him?

"Believe it sweetheart," RJ said in a menacing voice. "These are very valid concerns for my team and me. I appreciate the fact that you brought this opportunity to our attention, but we planned the heist. We're providing resources. We'll be taking the risks. There is still a day of the tournament left and our other guy has to make it to the final table. We really want him to make it, as it has less risk."

"So how do we know who to lose to?" Paul asked, his mind still going a hundred-miles-an-hour.

"I'm not going to tell you," RJ said. "We think if you just lose right away, our guy has a chance to move on with out you in the mix. Don't forget," he added, moving closer to the table. "If you don't lose like you've been ordered or if there are any leaks, to anybody, I'll deal with you both in a very serious manner."

"Wait a minute RJ," Paul said with as much authority as he could muster. "I don't understand your thinking. Let's assume we do what you want us to…"

"No Langley," RJ said, interrupting, narrowing his eyes even more, his face now contorted in a way that for instant even gave Paul pause. "Not an assumption. An order!"

"Hear me out, RJ," Paul said, hoping he sounded calmer than he felt. "Vivian and I will have already been noted as players and if what you say is right about our connection, what can having us lose accomplish? Seems to me that our participation in the tournament will mean we'll be questioned extensively by the authorities anyway if this heist comes off. A smart investigator will question every participant. They may think it strange that two of the most promising tournament entries bumbled their play the day before the fireworks. I'd think that Vivian and I would become prime suspects. Is that what you really want?"

"No, Langley that's not what we want," RJ said. "Let me run that line of thinking up the ladder."

Shit, thought Paul, he sounds like a bureaucratic businessman. Run it up the ladder, indeed.

Paul had been thinking about all this. His executive experience kicked in. He had to figure a way to identify RJ's player if he was to successfully thwart RJ's plan, and continue on to the final table and win it all fair and square. As for how he could successfully alert the police or hotel security still eluded him, but he had to make sure Vivian was safe.

"I think it's obvious we haven't yet played against your man." Paul said, determined to keep on the offensive. "Hell, Vivian and I haven't played against each other so far. But as the remaining participants fall by the wayside, the odds that we will play against each other tomorrow and your man as well are improved dramatically. What if I were to tell you that Vivian and I have a way to improve the odds of your man winning, if he plays against one or both of us?"

"Good idea Paul," Vivian said with such enthusiasm that he knew she had guessed where he was going with this.

"Go ahead;" said RJ, "I'm listening."

He did not, however, look as though he'd like what Paul was going to say. "First," Paul said. "If we do play against him and because of us advances to the final table, I think we should still get a cut of take."

Paul thought, that statement ought to convince that bastard that they were really serious about this, particularly since what he was about to propose would trick him into revealing the other player's identity. Then and only then, could he take the next step, and get Vivian the hell out of Vegas before all hell broke loose.

"Let me hear what you are talking about first," RJ said, eyes narrowed. "Then we'll talk."

"Like I said," Paul said. "I've come up with a way to transmit our pocket cards. It's fairly complex and only another player taught the system would get it."

"Okay," RJ said, lighting another cigarette. "So we could improve the odds. We'll need to have our man meet you both to go over this. And now is as good a time as any. "Get him," he ordered the less than attentive Alf. "And tell him to bring some chips and cards. We'll see what he has to say about this idea."

While Vivian went to powder her nose, RJ became confidential. "Vivian is a great lady. I'm sorry if I'm fucking up the chance for you to win the tournament. I know she's a very smart, and sometimes head strong woman, but this is dangerous shit and I don't want to see her get hurt."

Well, thought Paul, RJ gave him quite the opportunity to sound defeated. Come into my trap, you little shit.

"The last thing I want to you to do," Paul said. "Is to hurt Vivian in any way, but I think we'll live through all this." Even if you may not, thought Paul. "I just hope all this isn't so you can try and get her back?"

"Fuck you Langley," RJ said defiantly. "That's not it at all."

RJ clenched and unclenched his fists. He looked the quintessential hood.

Silence.

Paul thought that perhaps he had gone too far, and suddenly remembered how dangerous this guy could be, hoping the term "whacked" didn't come to RJ's mind. Paul couldn't wait to get on with the ruse, find out who RJ's other man was, play to win it all, without cheating and figure out, in detail, how to bring RJ down, with Vivian safely out of town.

RJ still looking furious and was about to continue to rip into Paul when Vivian returned. The groups' attempts at small talk, generally failed and the air was heavy with Paul's and RJ outbursts.

"Come on Vivian," Paul said. "I want to talk to you in private."

"Not so fast, you two," RJ said, as Paul and Vivian stood to leave.

"Jesus Christ, RJ," Vivian said defiantly. "Cool down. We need some private time. Besides, we need to make sure we can show your man our scheme correctly. It can be complicated and I need a refresher. Besides, I need some fresh air."

Damn, Vivian, Paul thought, *take it easy*. His warning glances to her had had no effect on her feistiness and the last thing he wanted was to send RJ into some rage.

"No," said RJ, "You both stay here." You can brush up on your scheme right here." Then turning to Alf, "how long before he gets here?"

"He said in about twenty-minutes or so," Alf answered.

"Fine, let's just relax and wait," RJ said and sat back in his chair, seemingly satisfied that his stern orders were going to be obeyed.

Paul spent the twenty-minuets or so that it took RJ's "new man" to arrive thinking of ways he could convince Vivian to take the first plane out of town. As far as he was concerned, however, that little shit, RJ, wasn't going to take the tourney away from him. He'd win it honestly and somehow he'd find a way to make sure that the entire two million was waiting for him when he did.

Small talk was impossible. The tension was thick and every few minutes or so, RJ would go over to Alf and whisper something, all the while glaring at Paul and Vivian who blurted expletives at no one in particular while Paul cast warning glances at her in vain.

By the time the man RJ wanted to replace them with arrived, a half hour later, Paul was having a difficult time containing his impatience and it was clear that Vivian was seething although, thankfully, she was now keeping her mouth shut.

When the other man, slightly overweight, and dressed in jeans and a tee shirt with the "Welcome to Fabulous Las Vegas" sign on his chest, entered the room carrying a small box, Paul recognized him as a very good player on the circuit and who had been the subject of several *Card Player* magazine articles. He gave Vivian and Paul a 'you look familiar' look.

"Hi RJ," he said. "What's up? I was just about to go to sleep when Alf called."

The man, who was introduced as Dee Goodwin, listened to what RJ had to say with droopy-eyed nonchalance that made it clear that the idea of taking part in grand larceny caused him no hesitation. After RJ explained that Vivian and Paul playing at the final table was too risky, Goodwin became considerably more alert when it was time for Paul and Vivian to show him how the shuffle worked.

Paul divided the chips and gave Vivian about half. He took the deck out of the box and gave them a quick shuffle.

Although she hadn't practiced the scheme very many times, Vivian started deftly playing with her stacks of chips just as if she would in a real game. Paul dealt her two cards and put the deck down. Vivian picked up her cards, showed them to Dee, and continued to play with her chips. Paul watched intently as Vivian went through the pattern. "Small pair." said Paul. Vivian turned over the cards. "Pair of sixes."

They repeated the demonstration several times until Paul saw a pair of jacks pattern. "Pair of jacks." Vivian flipped them over. "Pretty impressive," said Dee. "Let me see you do it, Paul. Vivian, you deal."

"Yes, that could help a player know what was in a person's pocket," Dee said after they had demonstrated the technique for about ten minutes. "I knew you were doing something, but I couldn't catch exactly how it worked. I think it has to do with those two chips and where you place them on the other stack, but I haven't seen it often enough to catch how you got the card value right. Another player would not know it was going on and might never notice. Did you think of this, Paul?"

"Yes, but we haven't had a chance to use it for real. We haven't played against each other. It only works for a low pair, without knowing the value or suits and specific cards over ten, still no suit."

"So what were you going to do with it?" Dee asked. "Just make sure one of you won and split the prize money?"

"Something like that," Vivian answered, her voice filled with boredom.

"We needed a way to guarantee that one of us got to the final table and you know why." Paul looked pointedly at RJ who was obviously very bored with the details of all this.

"I suppose it would help me," Dee said. "but I'm very good without it. I'm the guy that dumped Moneymaker yesterday. Still, I'll take any edge I can. It could be quite an edge now that I think about it. Why don't you show me how it works?"

"I'll be glad to, but first I need a number from RJ." Paul said, raising his voice.

"Okay, here's the deal." RJ sounded like he was in charge again. "If Dee here plays against one or both of you and advances to the final table and we pull this off, I'll give you fifty grand to split at that time."

Vivian nodded. "Okay," said Paul. "Let's show you how this works."

Showing the chip scheme to Dee had been easy enough and as Paul and Vivian rose to leave, RJ fired another warning shot. "You two follow my demands. I don't want any trouble from either of you. Make losing look good and I'd suggest you both get out of Vegas, as soon after that as possible.

Vivian turned to say something to RJ, but Paul pulled her away. "Okay RJ," Paul said. "We're outta here."

The ride back to the Four Queens was made in a relative silence as Paul and Vivian, still seething, found it difficult to start a conversation. Paul was determined now to get Vivian safely out of Vegas, early tomorrow morning if possible, and figure out how to thwart RJ's plan on his own. He loved this woman, and wanted her safe and sound, so they could continue the magic at a later time. Although, Paul thought, there was still tonight.

A few blocks from the hotel, Vivian broke the long silence. "It was a great idea," she said, "thinking of that chip scheme to find out who the other man was."

"Thanks," Paul said. "I wasn't sure how I'd find out otherwise. RJ surely wasn't just going to tell us. While you were in the restroom, I accused RJ of doing all this so that he could get you back."

"You didn't," Vivian said. "There's no way. He doesn't have a chance in hell. Isn't that obvious?"

"I sure did tell him and I was hoping you'd say that, but we need to have him believe we're going to obey him although it pisses us off. I figured once we found out who this other guy is, I can beat him legitimately, and figure out how to stop him."

Hoping Vivian didn't respond to his 'I can beat him' comment and not 'we,' Paul hoped to wait until they were safely in their room to tell her that she needed to get out of Vegas in the morning.

"I've been giving that some thought too," Vivian said. "Maybe – no, not maybe - when we get to the final table, assuming that Dee makes it, too, we need to figure out how to stop that son-of-a-bitch."

"Let's wait to finish discussing this until were in the room," Paul said as the BMW slid into the Valet area. "I need to tell you something really important."

As Paul helped her out of the car, Vivian was beaming, as if she expected that he was going to tell her something really romantic. Knowing that he was probably going to hate him when he told her that she had to leave, Paul smiled back. At least now he knew that he was really in love with her. When they were settled in the two easy chairs with a glass of wine each, Paul took in a deep breath, and looked directly into her beautiful green eyes. "Vivian," he said, "I care about you more than you know. In fact, I love you. And for that reason, I'm going to tell you something you're not going to like."

"What?" Vivian said voice full of concern. "That you are really pissed off that I brought you into this mess? Well I ..."

"No," it's not that," Paul said, not letting her finish. "It's that I'm very concerned for your safety and what that bastard may do. I think it's best if you get on a plane early tomorrow morning and get home before that crackpot screws up our lives entirely. I'll stay here and figure out a way to foil his plans and keep us safe, but you need to be gone. I need you in my life afterwards."

Vivian eased out of her chair and slid to floor, resting her arms on Paul's lap. "Well, Langley," she said and he saw that her eyes were full of tears. "I don't know what to say. I love you too, but you've got another think coming if you believe for a minute that I'm leaving you here to deal with this all by yourself. If we're going to be partners, we going to deal with this as a team. I feel so responsible for all this, no matter what you say, I'm going to stay and help you figure out something. Besides," Vivian continued as she rose and leaned down to kiss him, "I love you, too, and if you think I could even stand to not be here when all this goes down worried to death about you, then maybe…"

"Okay," Paul said, not letting her finish. "I can't force you to leave, but hear me out. My concern is that, at that point in the tournament, if we haven't lost, as RJ has demanded, he may do something drastic."

"Like what?" Vivian said voice full of genuine concern.

"I'm not sure," Paul said. "But because we're still playing at the final table, he could decide to call it off on his own because of the risks, or he could somehow threaten us the night before. I just don't know, but we need to continue to think about all the possibilities. And for now we need to keep up the appearance of being willing to cheat to help Goodwin and have RJ assume we're going to lose and be gone on the fifth."

Paul found himself wishing he never should have said to Vivian, 'I'd rather plan a robbery.' Can't, would've, should've, he scolded himself, but he still wished this would all end soon, with Vivian and him at the final table, winning it all and RJ gone somehow.

"Oh, Paul," Vivian said. "I've been thinking about how dangerous this could be. I'm not sure how to go against the family. It will be dangerous. I know these guys."

"I don't really think it's a family matter." Paul said. "From what I know about the Mafia, they're not grab-the-money-in-broad-daylight kind of people, I think it's just RJ's plan and he's doing it for you. He'd like to win you back."

"I told you, *no way*." Vivian stroked Paul's cheek. "He's a crook and he's doing it because it's the way he is. He can't get me back no matter what and he knows it. As much as I hate to say it, he's *dangerous* and I think we ought to be very careful. We're two bright people, we can come up with something safe don't you think? I guess if we don't think of incredibly secure, promise me we'll do as he asks. There'll always be other tournaments."

"No way, Vivian," Paul said, his voice rising in pitch and intensity. "We just decided to fuck RJ and win the tournament. I'm just not going to let that little bastard get away with it no matter what his motives are. We're too good at poker to stop on a voluntary basis. If we get beat, we get beat, but it's not because he forced us too. I promise to think of something that will be safe."

"I will too," Vivian added and pulled him to a standing position. They kissed deeply. Their lovemaking was intense and unsettling at the same time. Paul did not know for sure what was going to happen and he only knew he had to make sure Vivian was safe.

Removing his watch to place it on the nightstand, Paul saw the little electronic device still taped to the back. That little shit, RJ, wasn't so meticulous after all. *Okay,* Paul thought, *let me think on that.*

CHAPTER 18

THE ESPN INTERVIEWS had been easy enough for them. Walking through the casino together, Paul felt a renewed confidence about moving toward that final table where they saw some of the bigger names that were still in the tournament, including their new archenemy, Dee. Only Scotty Nguyen, the favorite to win now, Michael Ross and Roxanne Rhodes stood near the entrance, waiting to enter. Both Vivian and Paul were on edge wondering whom they would be facing in the first round. They examined the blind and ante values for the day:

LEVEL	ANTE	BLINDS
1ST	$2,000	$1600-$3200
2ND	$2,000	$1600-$3200
3RD	TBD	TBD
4TH	TBD	TBD
5TH	TBD	TBD
6TH	TBD	TBD
7TH	TBD	TBD

MINIMUM BET - $5,000

PLAY FOR LEVELS 3 AND ON WILL BE DETERMINED AFTER ANALYSIS OF PLAYER AND CHIP COUNTS.

ALL PLAY WILL END TODAY WHEN THE FINAL SEVEN PLAYERS ARE DETERMINED. PLEASE NOTE THIS MAY BE EARLY OR VERY LATE. PLAY TOMORROW (THE FINAL DAY) WILL COMMENCE AT NOON.

Paul settled into his seat number two at table number four. Vivian had table three and Paul could make out Dee at table five. Not having to face each other yet meant luck was with them right now. Paul hoped the cards would be as lucky. The lights the TV crew had brought in made the room, with its mirrored columns, glitter. The tables were surrounded by a garland of rope lights attached to the barrier, separating the players from the audience. The Four Queens logo, in gold stitching on red velvet panels, hung from the barrier at every other eight-foot section. The section for spectators and press had been enlarged, taking up the space previously occupied by poker tables. When the other players joined his table, the announcer cleared his throat and began.

"Good afternoon ladies and gentlemen and poker players from around the world. Welcome to the second to last day of the Four Queens first annual Big Stakes Poker Tournament. This is certainly going to be an exciting day as the remaining thirty-four players vie for a spot at the final table. Here it is. Table number one. Tomorrow two million dollars in cash will be stacked beside it. How's that for an incentive?"

The crowd responded with a smattering of applause and soft cheers. The players, on the other hand, restrained themselves, clearly wanting to get on with it.

"Okay," he continued, sounding to Paul's ears, at least, like a slot tournament announcer. "Let's get started and the best of luck to you all."

Facing his competition for the next level or so, Paul estimated the chip stacks and decided he was first or second in chip count. A nondescript woman he hadn't seen before, sitting opposite him in seat six, seemed to have the short stack. At the two thousand dollar ante, if she didn't win a pot in the next five hands, the big blind of $3200 would eliminate her.

"Players ante please," said the dealer, and off they went.

Paul pushed in his ante and small blind and picked up his first pair of cards, eight and J of clubs. The action went around the table. Call, call, fold, fold, fold. Small blind in seat one called, and tipped in his required chips. Pot's right.

The three community cards dealt out. Four of clubs, seven of diamonds, deuce of hearts. Paul checked and so did the others. The turn was a five of diamonds, and the river, a nine of hearts, was all free to the players after another two rounds of checking. A pair of jacks, held by young man wearing a long sleeve Nike shirt with a Nike hat won the small pot.

Play continued, with chips seesawing back and forth between the four remaining players. The nondescript woman, whom Paul learned was Elizabeth from Dallas, and two other 'newbie's' lost graciously enough and left the table. With just an hour into play, Paul estimated the total number of players to be fewer than twenty-eight. Paul couldn't wait to play against Vivian who, her red hair cascading about her shoulders was lost in total concentration at her table across the room. However, that time shouldn't come too early on, or they wouldn't both make it to the final table.

The announcer never seemed to stop. Paul found it annoying. ESPN crews continued their coverage, trying to be present whenever an "all-in" occurred. Paul assumed the players at table one, where the pocket cameras were being analyzed to death by the coverage 'experts' in the media room. He was relieved when the first break came after two hours of intense play.

"Shit, Paul," Vivian told him when they met one another in the casino. "I took out two players who called my all-in. I had a pair of cowboys and flopped a set before the turn. The flop had a pair of tens and a king. I was feeling very confident even when I was called even though the guy could have had a pair of tens in the pocket. I could've been done. All three of us stood up and waited for the turn and the river." Vivian pulled hard on her cigarette. "The turn had nothing, so I was sure I was done. I was looking over in your direction and praying. God! A king dropped in the river. Can you believe it? It was so exciting!"

"That's great Vivian," Paul told her. It occurred to him that this was where the excitement was, doing it on your own. No tricks. No heist. No RJ. Just pure talent and love of the game. "What did the other guy have?"

"He was looking for a straight,"Vivian told him. "A pure gut shot. I just don't know why he called with a pair of tens showing. It was just so fucking great. I have the chip lead at my table now!"

"An interesting scenario may develop very soon," Paul said in a low voice. "What if Dee gets dumped on his own? It could happen. Then what do you suppose RJ would do? I guess he'd have to drop the whole thing, or proceed with something else, probably set off the fireworks from the audience?"

"If he does, it will be even more chaotic, but at this point I don't give a shit." Vivian said grimly. "I guess now I'm hoping Dee loses and one of us can win the tournament. That will serve RJ right. We'll show him."

"It is going to be dangerous to be at the final table,"Paul reminded her. "God knows how RJ is going to detonate a cylinder. Let's see how the next few hours go."

Vivian was still saying all the right things, thought Paul, and like him, remained steadfast, apparently deciding that the game is the exciting thing, not the heist or part of RJ's money. But he knew that she wanted to clobber Dee, and move to the final table, thwarting the plan. Paul had an inkling of an idea. He'd let in permeate a while.

As they were returning to the room, a *Card Player Magazine* reporter asked to have a few words with Vivian, and scribbled furiously as Vivian described her hand and feelings about her four kings. Only then did Paul realize that Vivian had dumped Scotty Nguyen, probably the best known, and the leading money winner on the circuit.

The officials decided that play was progressing well and only made one change to the minimum bet:

THE NEXT TWO HOURS OF PLAY – MINIMUM BET $25000

3RD	**$5000**	**$16000-$32000**
4TH	**$5000**	**$16000-$32000**

NORMAL BREAK AFTER LEVEL 4.

REMINDER: AFTER LEVEL 5, THERE WILL BE AN HOUR AN A HALF DINNER BREAK.

The officials created seat assignments based on player's chip counts. Most of the big name players were assigned to table one, probably for the benefit of the ESPN crew, the members of which had placed two cameras on tripods, book ending the table. Three new players were assigned seats at Paul's table. "Fresh Meat" thought Paul. He was feeling very confident. They still had sizable stacks of chips. One of the tables had been removed and the barrier now circled the remaining four tables, giving the players more of an-in-a-pit feeling.

Paul was relieved to see that Vivian and Dee were still at separate tables, although he was not sure if he felt this was a good or bad sign. If all three of them lost, it could be fun seeing how RJ pulls off the plan. If Dee lost without playing Vivian or him, Paul knew RJ would have to think of something desperate or hopefully, abandon the whole thing. But, he reminded himself, he didn't care about

RJ and his plan to share. He didn't want a dime of RJ's ill-gotten money even in the very unlikely case he pulled it off.

The green felt tabletop displayed the blinds and antes, while the dealer dealt out the first round of cards. Paul kept telling himself not to do anything stupid. He had plenty of chips and his strategy was to simply advance. He reminded himself if he had to lose, it wouldn't be by choice even if he faced Dee and or Vivian.

Over the next two hours, it seemed that the remaining players had the same thought. Play was moving slowly and even though the large blinds and antes were chewing up chips, only two players were eliminated. Even the public address announcer gave up trying to promote excitement. Then, just before dinner break, Paul received a J and ace of spades. He called the big blind and incredibly, so did the entire table. It was a $125,000 pot, before the flop.

Flip. Flip. Flip. Paul was staring at a six, K and ten of spades. He had flopped a 'nut' flush. He waited. Big blind checked. Next position raised $40,000. Paul thought the raiser was trying to buy the pot. He looked at the man who had tipped in forty, one-thousand black chips. He was wearing an "All In" shirt and matching ball cap with a matching slogan on the bill.

Paul quickly calculated the odds. All In probably had pocket kings or even a pair of spades. In any case, Paul would take him with his ace high flush. If he had kings and the turn and/or river contained a king, Paul would lose it. Paul could flop a royal if the Q of spades dropped. He sized up the various chip stacks. Paul called and reraised $40,000.

It was obvious that Paul's reraise had the table thinking. They had all invested in the pot, and it was sizable. Folding would be difficult for many players, but at this level, one couldn't afford to chase the next two cards. Unless of course, one was desperate. Two players called. Two others folded. All In looked at Paul for a sign. Paul just stared back at him over his granny glasses and rifled his chips.

"You wouldn't have an ace of spades with another spade in there would you?" All In asked him. It was clearly a rhetorical question. "I should call and then bet on the turn and then reraise you," he added. "That would be the smart thing to do, but you know what? Read my shirt."

Paul already knew he was going to call him and asked the dealer to count the chips. All In had put in another $228,000. Paul counted out his $228,000, and pushed in his chips. "Call." Paul had about $75,000 remaining in chips, not out, but short stacked in this game if he lost. The remaining two participants looked at their stacks of chips, nervously. "Hell, there's a million hands that can beat me," one of them said. "I fold." The other man agreed.

All In flipped over his cards and stood up. As Paul had suspected, he had a pair of kings. Paul flipped over his high spades and rose to tower over him. The dealer aligned the hands on the table and buried a card.

"Come on, king," All In begged.

The dealer flipped over a seven of diamonds before burying another card and producing a queen of clubs. "Damn, look at that," someone said looking at Paul's ace high straight and flush. "He almost got the royal."

All In circled the table to congratulate Paul, negotiating his way around the ESPN cameraman to shake hands. Paul felt the perspiration running down his forehead. "Thanks," was all he could muster as he paced around, watching the dealer slide all the chips into his corner. Paul now had well over $600,000 in chips, not the lead in the tournament, but perhaps enough to keep playing through the evening, which meant he would certainly be moving tables, perhaps facing Dee and or Vivian and be in splendid position to make the final table.

At the dinner break, Paul suggested to Vivian they just get a pizza and retreat to the room to discuss their strategy.

"You know, Vivian," Paul said taking a bite of pizza. "We've got a few things to worry about. If one of us faces Dee tonight, he'll be expecting us to provide the chip signals. My concern is that if we don't, he'll manage to get word to RJ, and God knows what that little shit will do."

"Yes," Vivian said, "I thought about that too. If it came to me, I figure I'll just shuffle my chips in any old manner, and if need be, just say he was too slow to pick it up. You don't really think it will come to that do you?"

"We can't be too careful," Paul said. "Here's what I think could happen tonight and tomorrow. One, or both of us will face Dee and we'll kick his ass, which will probably result in some sinister threat from RJ. On the other hand, if he wins, then we're left with one of us gone, and the other going to the final table with him. Third case scenario all three of us play well enough to get to the final table. Then we're faced with dealing with the whole gas bomb nonsense, assuming that Dee will detonate it as required. It could be the same under scenario two, if one of us is at the final table with him."

"There's a fourth possibility," Vivian said, frowning. "We have RJ's cell phone number. We can call him and make up some excuse about how we think that our chip-telling scheme is likely to be observed, that we won't be using it. We could tell him that we understand it means we don't get our cut but that's just the way it has to be. Then if we beat Dee, we're off the hook."

"That could work," Paul told her. "But you know what, sweetheart, I'd really just love to beat Dee, no cheating, and figure a way to stop

RJ, so we can win all the money and there's only a couple of ways to do that. We call the cops and tell them we heard about the plot and they could be ready to jump in and stop it. Doing that could be safer in the short term, but unless they manage to arrest the little weasel, it won't be safe in the long run. He'd track us down. You heard what he said."

"Why do you think RJ would suspect us of turning him in?" Vivian asked.

"Well, let's think about it," Paul said. "Right now he thinks we're pissed off because he told us we're not the ones to drop the cylinder and won't get our share. And he knows how upset we are that he told us to lose. Sure, he'll think it's us. Who else?"

"My God, I think you're right," Vivian said, her voice rising. "So what was the other possibility?"

Paul and Vivian continued to debate the merits of each scenario. The pros and cons were thoroughly examined along with the risks of each particular option. A situation that would make RJ blame Dee for the failure of the cylinder to detonate was examined carefully as was another possibility about just losing and skipping town before all the turmoil began. They both agreed that any plan that involved one or both of them not playing up to their potential and winning it all was unacceptable. It finally came down to a just a few options. Poker was almost their second life and anything that would jeopardize the fulfilling of their long held dream to win a major tournament had been discarded, quickly. Finally, in agreement as to what they would do, "The only way this works" Paul concluded, "is for you and or me to be at that final table with Dee. No other scenario is as safe, in my opinion."

"I need to continue to think about it," Vivian said. "I think you're right though, as don't like any of our other options at this point.

Actually, I definitely do not want to skip town. I want to kick yours and Dee's ass."

"Wanna make a side bet?" Paul said, grinning.

"Sure," said Vivian, her voice returning to the huskiness, Paul loved so much. "Winner gets to choose whatever they want."

"You're on," Paul said, "And one more thing to think about," he added. "If we find that one or both of us is at the final table tonight, we should consider packing, and being ready to leave town right after the tournament. I don't want to face RJ or his thugs if we spoil his plan, and if he manages to create some havoc in an attempt to grab the money, I'd just as soon be gone when all the questioning starts, if we can."

"Oh Paul," Vivian said, "I thought we were going to spend some more time together?"

"We will," Paul said, "But it may not be in the next few days. I promise."

As they finished their pizza and prepared to return to the evening session, Paul thought he'd better continue to think of ways to improve or modify their plan, even though his confidence in Vivian's loyalty was growing by leaps and bounds, he wasn't sure he'd share everything with Vivian. Not yet. Perhaps, although he hated to think it possible, not ever.

CHAPTER 19

THE FACE-TO-FACE CONFRONTATIONS Paul had been expecting, one that he knew it would be quite interesting with Dee was now sitting at Vivian's table. Before sizing up his own new competition, Paul noted that Dee appeared to have slightly more chips than Vivian did. From Paul's vantage point, he could see the back of Vivian's head and Dee's profile and was surprised to discover how much it bothered him that he could only watch helplessly as they played.

Paul did a quick head count around the room and tried to remember the prize schedule. He knew he and Vivian were in the ten thousand dollar range of players twenty through thirty. If a few more players left before they did, the prize money would probably hit twenty grand. The final table was where the real money was and right now he was positive that either he or she would make it. At this point, they at least had more than their expenses covered.

Play started. For the first few hands, Paul received no usable cards. The next half a dozen hands or so, he won a few relatively small pots. Paul was surprised that the officials hadn't cranked up the blinds to eat away chips at a faster clip although, of course they could still do that later on in the evening.

Just as Paul folded on some muck, a commotion occurred at Vivian's table. Two players stood up, one of them Dee. It was obviously an "all in." Vivian was still seated, but Paul couldn't see if she was in on the action or not. As an ESPN cameramen circled the table, Paul stood up to observe the action. Dee and a man wearing a completely out-of-place-for Vegas ski sweater had their chips stacked in the pot and stood ready for the flop. Vivian turned around, and winked at Paul. She had folded. The audience leaned over the barrier and some stood up. The announced tried to add to the tension. Paul could just make out the community and Sweater Man's cards, but couldn't see Dee's. Sweater Man had a pair of kings. The three card flop, A, J, seven. The table broke into chatter, waiting the turn. The turn and river came in short order. Seven and four. Sweater Man slumped down and Dee raised his arms in victory. As the announcer went on inanely about the last casualty, Paul took a moment to see what was going on at Vivian's table. Dee had won all of Sweater Man's chips with three aces, but the height of Vivian's stack of chips, decided that she was still in great position to move on.

Paul returned to his seat, and wondered how Vivian had managed to accumulate more chips, as the play at her table had been relatively quiet until that last hand. Looking at his watch, he realized that he wouldn't know for an hour or so at the next break. The next hour passed quickly, as several players left the remaining four tables, including two from table one.

Paul wiped out another player at his table with a second flush, something that happened so often during the last hour that the others were calling him "flush man." When the break was finally announced, the tournament was down to the final twenty-one players.

When they were seated at their usual video poker machines, Vivian told Paul, that she had won two really large pots from Dee, once with just a pair of kings. "I'm shuffling my chips in a random manner," she said, "but I think he's ignoring me after he messed up. He's thinking he's not catching on fast enough. So what do you think? Do you think Dee will complain to RJ that we're not playing the way we're supposed to?"

"Not yet," Paul said. "He won't complain about it, unless he gets dumped and doesn't get to the final table. We'll have to see if he is bumped up to table one after the break. He had a lot of chips, so he might. How's your chip count? I have the chip lead at my table now."

"I don't know exactly," Vivian admitted. "I think I'm in second or third place behind Dee. I didn't check the master list. Hell, you may make it to table one before Dee. What would you do if you did?"

"I'll continue to play my ass off and wait for you and Dee to join me," Paul said, full of confidence.

"Okay," Vivian said, "Let's go and kick butt."

"Right on," Paul replied, "Just at the moment, everything is going our way, and maybe, just maybe this will all have a happy ending. Let's go get 'em."

But, secretly, he was not that confident. The only way there would be a happy ending to all this was if that SOB and his entire gang are locked up forever.

Happy ending indeed, thought Paul, as he led her back to the action. Just how was he really going to make it all happen? It would only be happy if he could pull this off.

The tournament officials had not changed the blinds or antes. Paul and Vivian circled the remaining three tables to see where their chips were placed. As Paul had suspected, Dee had been assigned table one, while Vivian and he were still at separate tables. "Okay," Paul whispered to Vivian. "So he doesn't have any reason to complain to RJ. Now it's time we got to the final table too."

It was now up to Dee to remain at table one. If he lost now, Paul or Vivian could do nothing about it. Vivian and he were playing beautifully, but still had several pots to win before advancing. Meanwhile, it made Paul feel good that he and Vivian hadn't had to cheat to get Dee to win.

The announcer droned on about the twenty-one finalists, trying to guess who would be standing as the final seven tonight or early tomorrow morning. With that, play started. Recognizing many of the name players scattered around the four remaining tables, Paul went into his memory banks, pulling up some helpful traits and player patterns that would prove helpful in any showdowns. He was amused at the variety of dress as he always had been, but this bunch looked quite differently, everything from plain tee shirts and shorts, to long sleeve shirts. Half the men wore the latest style sunglasses. It appeared Vivian was the lone female contestant remaining. Probably because of that, as well as her extraordinary beauty, ESPN covered her continuously.

Half an hour later, Paul was looking at the flop of eight, nine, ten off suit, and was considering the raise of $30,000 from Wrap Around Sunglasses at the end of the table. To call or not to call? He looked at his pocket of suited seven, and Q. With two outs, he had a possible straight looming. He was feeling good about the river and turn. However, if he called, it would be considered poor play. And then he needed to lay pipe, as it were.

Still contemplating the two outs for a straight - slim and slimmer. "Call." The turn and river did not produce a six or a J. Paul watched Sunglasses rake in his chips.

Two hands later, Paul was dealt a pair of sevens. He was in late position so he watched the action come around to him prior to the flop. The man immediately to his right covered his face down pocket cards and peeked at them for the second or third time. Normally this was a sign of weakness, but this man maybe trying to "tell" a weakness from a strong hand.

Paul watched from the corner of his eye as the man counted out his chips and said, "All in." Without looking at his pocket cards again, he called. Paul decided that this guy was bluffing, or at least had a high pair.

When the rest of the table folded, the man to Paul's his right stood up. Paul remained seated as the dealer counted out his chips, a substantial number. It was clear that his lead had certainly increased in the last hour or so. The dealer sent some chips back to the Paul. "Okay, the pot is right," the dealer said.

"Jeez you can't be working on another flush," the remaining player complained, pacing around nervously.

"Hell," Paul said as turned over a pair of sevens and the other man disclosed an ace, K, of diamonds. "You're closer to a flush than I am."

Cheering and oohhhs and aahs rumble around the room as Paul rakes in the huge pile of chips. Incredibly, the flop was an off suited three, seven, and an eight, and the turn and river held and eight and Q. Paul had three sevens. *Damn*, Paul thought, *I'm on a hell of a streak.*

Looking around at the tables, he saw only two vacant spots, the one recently vacated at Vivian's table and the other to the right of him. As play continued, Paul's resolve to continue to play well became more intense. Vivian seems to be doing as well; at least she was still there with plenty of chips. Having been dealt a J, and a ten of clubs on the next hand, Paul found himself on the big blind. Five players called. The flop came, a four, deuce, and K, unsuited. Paul folded.

During the next half hour of play after the break, Paul won several small pots. Every time he would raise or attempt an all-in ploy, his opponents would fold. Clearly, his reputation was preceding him. As for Vivian, he saw her walking to table one, carrying a load of chips, ready to face Dee again.

In the next hand, Paul received a pair of tens. Two rounds of raises before the flop increased the pot to well over $400,000, and he knew that that now was the time to scare off some folks. But he'll need some luck on the flop.

Before the flop, the table looked to Paul to call or reraise as he had done the previous two rounds. Instead, he announced, "All-in," and moved his chips to the dealer to count. At the same time, two players called. Well, shit, he hadn't scared anybody off, has he?" However, both the man in a plain purple tee shirt and the man wearing a Nordstrom Façonnable long sleeve shirt didn't look very certain about his call now. Waiting for the flop, Paul flips over his pair of tens, Purple Shirt turned over a pair of jacks, and Nordstrom Shirt donned an ace and Q of clubs.

Amazingly, the flop, turn and river, were a ten, deuce, trey, A, and K, giving Paul a win with a set of tens. Another player gone, leaving Purple Shirt without enough for the small blind.

The next half an hour was a big blur as far as Paul was concerned. He only knew that he was ushered to table one and that the showdown with Dee and Vivian he had so desperately wanted was now about to happen. The thought of RJ "getting even" if Paul or Vivian beat Dee, absorbed him as he stacks his chips at the table he dreamed about often.

Wired with a lapel microphone, Paul faced Dee who is seated in position one and Vivian, who was seated at the end of the table, with whom he traded smiles. The empty table that Paul had so effectively wiped out by his playing skill, and some very good luck was moved out of the way by a Four Queens' crew and only three players remained at table two. The final seven players would be decided very soon.

With only three players remaining at table two and Paul facing Vivian at table one, he was suddenly aware that he was on an incredible high which consisted of the sense of triumph that came with having made it this far, mixed with an awareness that, sometime in the next hour or so, his life and Vivian's would be in danger. Because unless everything went as planned, RJ would see that they were both eliminated. Paul had no doubts on that score. They were here because they had to be. And he was determined that he was going to make it pay. And that meant more than the two million. It meant that soon, RJ was going to be out of their lives forever.

The trouble was that Dee's pile seemed to match his. Damn RJ and his plot. What he really wanted was to be able to concentrate on this game and afterward on Vivian. If there was anything he didn't want to look forward to was canisters exploding and the possibility that he and Vivian might end up dead.

CHAPTER 20

THE ANNOUNCER WHEELED his cordless microphone around the table and introduced the players at the first table, starting with position one. Circling the table, and he placed his hand on each player's shoulder in turn:

From St. Louis, Missouri - Dee Goodwin.

From Dallas, Texas - Kenna James.

From Right here in Las Vegas - Don Hart.

From Auburn, California - Paul Langley.

From Phoenix, Arizona - Scott Epstein.

From Rockford, Illinois - Vivian Davis.

From Santa Cruz, California - Kenny Wagner.

There was a smattering of applause as each player's name along with their chip counts, echoed across the room, the Vegas entry appearing, understandably, to have the largest contingent of fans.

"Ok, gentlemen and lady," the announcer said. "Start your engines. Dealers, deal a way."

As the dealer reminded the players to reveal their hole cards to the little cameras buried in the table's rail, Paul eagerness, coupled with the rush of adrenalin had him as poised and ready as he'd ever been. Vivian looked just as focused.

After mixing the cards and shuffling the cards, the dealer buried the top card and dealt. Paul looked directly at Dee as the cards were flayed around the table and at the same time casually reordering his chips. Showing the corners of his cards to the camera and looking at them at the same time was a new maneuver to him, but he soon got the hang of it. He threw in his muck, an unsuited four, and six.

A few hands later, Paul anted and placed his big blind in the pot, receiving a pair of ten's. Hah! He thought, read that, as he caught Dee staring at the way he was stacking and playing with his chips, trying to read some meaning into it. Only the TV crew on the second floor and Paul knew what he was holding when Dee and Vivian both folded. Scott Epstein called the big blind and reraised $50,000. Which meant, Paul figured, that he must think Paul had his tens beaten. Small blind folded and Hart, from Vegas appeared to be contemplating his options. "Call," he said finally, and Paul followed suit.

After the flop of Q, ten, nine, unsuited, Paul checked to Epstein who looked at Hart and announced all-in. Paul watched Hart play with his chips before finally calling.

Shit, Paul thought. Vivian as watching closely, both elbows on the table, eyes riveted on the action. What was he supposed to do now? He had a set of tens with two chances, or outs to a straight, while Hart and Epstein Dee probably had trip queens or trip nines, and maybe a pair of aces between them somewhere. All his instincts and good poker sense said to fold.

"Call," announced Paul, asking the dealer for a chip count.

Idly fingered his remaining chips, Paul realized that, if he lost this hand, he wouldn't be near the chip lead as Hart flipped over his pair of queens. Then when Paul revealed his pair of tens, Epstein slowly turned over his pair of nines. What was Epstein playing with those for, thought Paul? Hell, for that matter, why the hell was he playing with just a pair of tens? Hart's trip K's were the odds on favorite right now. Hart would be gone, and Paul severely wounded if Epstein won this one, both of them would be short stacked. If Paul won, both men would be gone, neither of them with enough chips for the blind. Paul imagined the TV commentators analyzing the play of all three of them and they were probably being very critical of their play up to now.

The turn and river took forever to drop. Ace of diamonds. Ten of clubs! The next few moments were another big blur to Paul. He remembered shaking hands with Hart and Epstein and hearing Vivian say, "Way to go Paul!"

Before the commotion of his win died down, the two remaining players from table two were introduced. Before the dealer could start another round of play, the announcer declared an end to the play for the day in a booming voice. The seven finalists, he said were set for the big showdown at noon tomorrow.

Big showdown, indeed, thought Paul, as he and Vivian counted their chips, signed the forms, and avoided Dee's icy stare.

Later in their room, the wine poured and music playing, Paul decided to include Vivian in his plan. She paced around the room as he told her what he planned to do. Paul hoped she bought his line of reasoning and plan of action including how he had calculated that he could reduce the risk of RJ's potential retribution. For what seemed a long while, Vivian remained silent. *Read my mind Vivian*, Paul thought. *You know I'm right.*

"You really think it will work?" Vivian said, finally, "Yes, and we're not going to answer the door or the phone," Paul warned her. "I tell you, I think it will work but it will take perfect timing, but I think I can do it." Paul tapped on his watch. "And the quicker we're gone afterwards, the better."

"Okay," Vivian said, "You're probably right. But please promise you'll be careful. I love you!"

And then she grinned and he knew that she was all he had ever needed. Now, if only they could stay alive.

CHAPTER 21

AFTER BREAKFAST AND a rousing shower together, Paul and Vivian packed most of their belongings ready for a quick departure after the tournament. Their fears about the day remained bottled up, due, perhaps, to the fact that they knew precisely what they were going to do. Now all they had to do was to remain buoyant and determined to focus on the game. Until, that is, it was time to do otherwise. Over forty-five minutes early, they made their way to the tournament room to have a sneak peek, both dressed as professionally as possible without over doing it. Vivian was wearing a green skirt, and white blouse, her hair in a matching green bandana while   Paul wore crisp Levis and a long sleeve white shirt; the cuffs folded two turns up his arms Chinos and his New Balance sneakers, a late addition to his wardrobe to make sure he was prepared for action.

The tournament officials had not changed the blinds and antes for the final day, as it turned out and perhaps, given what was going to happen, they wouldn't need to. At all events, the final day could go on for many hours until a final victor emerged. Several workers were placing "Cinco de Mayo" posters around the lobby and poker room and additional guards seemed to be posted around or maybe it was just Paul noticing them by his knowledge of the 'event' in less than hour.

Names, hometowns, and chip counts of the finalists were posted on a big board.

$315,000. Paul Langley – Auburn, California.

$245,000. Dee Goodwin – St. Louis, Missouri.

$210,000. Vivian Davis – Rockford, Illinois.

$170,000. Kenna James – Dallas, Texas.

$145,000. O'Dell Sisson – San Antonio, Texas

$135,000. Felix Rodriguez – San Diego, California.

$80,000. Kenny Wagner – Santa Cruz, California.

"Christ, Look at that!" Vivian exclaimed to Paul. "You have the chip lead. That was a hell of a pot at the end."

"Yes," Paul agreed, "and that son of a bitch, Dee, isn't that far behind or too far ahead of you. This is anybody's tournament to win."

After killing some time in the casino, trying to relax by playing a little Keno, Paul and Vivian found their seats at the table, under a new bank of lights. It was no wonder, Paul thought, that those guys on TV and some here, always wore sunglasses. It wasn't just an affectation!

Watching Dee approach the table, Paul couldn't help but look down at his pant leg, trying to see some evidence of the cylinder dangling there. No sign! Was he carrying it? Or had the plan been called off?

As the seven finalists stood or sat around making idle chatter while they waited to begin, Dee sat staring into space, folding and unfolding his arms. Trading glances with Vivian, Paul told himself that although Dee might be a skilled, straight-faced poker player, as a soon-to-be-criminal he was demonstrating that he was either apprehensive, nervous, preoccupied, or worried. Probably all four. Had he, Paul wondered, already dropped the cylinder?

Suddenly the lights came up, and ESPN cameramen began swiveling their cameras, and the announcer grabbed the microphone. Conversation ceased between the players as they took their respective places, waiting for the pomp and circumstance of the final day to begin.

After each of the finalists' names and chip counts was announced there was a smattering of applause, followed by some prerecorded music with a national anthem flavor to it as four armed guards entered the room, with cameramen following, each carrying a bank bag, all of which they emptied on the table, creating mounds of hundred dollar bills.

Hot damn, Paul thought, *that was a lot of cash. Thank God, they're going to win and not steal it.* Dee, who was sitting across from Paul, didn't even look at it while the announcer droned on about the cash and how exciting all this was.

The four guards took their places behind the table on which the cash was piled, facing the audience. Paul wondered where else other guards might be positioned and whether they were uniformed or in plain clothes. Not that it mattered to him any more, but the window of opportunity was now open to RJ, although Paul wasn't sure whether or not the cash would remain in full view, perhaps until the last of the seven was declared the winner. According to the letter from the Four Queens, each player that was eliminated from now on would be treated to a small ceremony, including a picture. If Dee and RJ's gang were going to strike, it should be well before the first player was eliminated.

A red-jacketed security man, standing on the other side of the velvet rope garland behind Dee, made eye contact with Paul and nodded slightly.

After thanking the many sponsors of the event and mentioning the Four Queens way too many times, the announcer finally ended with the clichés Paul hated, "Are you ready?" and, "May the best person win."

Once all the player's antes and blinds were in place, the dealer passed out the first hand. Paul looked at his watch, not even noting the time, and picked up his first two cards.

A four and six, unsuited. He folded.

Vivian called the big blind and small blind called as well. Pot's right. Bury. Deal the flop, J, eight and four, unsuited. Vivian won the small pot with trip J's.

The next hour of play were like a heavyweight-boxing match in the early rounds, each player feigning and dodging around, sizing up their opponents, waiting for an opportunity to deliver a blow, while the blinds, ate up their resources as time wore out boxers.

Soon, Kenna James from Dallas, wearing aviator sunglasses and a khaki safari shirt, raised $80,000, nearly half his chips, after the flop.

Paul and all the others except Vivian had folded. Without hesitation, Vivian pushed in the required chips and said, "Call."

That a baby, thought Paul. The flop contained a J of diamonds, nine of clubs, eight of clubs. James, looked surprised that he had been called, and so quickly. After burning a card, the dealer flipped out the turn, a nine of diamonds. James hesitated, and looked at his pocket cards again.

"Check," James said knocking on the table.

Oh boy, thought Paul, James is running in to Vivian's trap.

"All in," announced Vivian, just as Paul thought she would, but wasn't sure what her pocket contained. Pair of jacks?

If James could have taken back his original $80,000 bet, he would have, Paul thought. Fiddling with his chips, James kept looking at Vivian and then his pocket cards. "Fold," he finally said, in frustration. Vivian raked in her big pot, still not offering an expression, or telling James, in spite of his begging, what she held.

A few hands later, short stacked Kenny Wagner, looking tired and disheveled in his plain green tee shirt, and ugly purple baseball cap, went all in against James and lost. The final table was now down to five. The announcer was now keeping a chip count tally for the audience and Paul was still in the lead, followed by Vivian, who kept looking daggers at him, had only $10k less than he. Paul was watching for Vivian to make a move, when he felt the tingling of electricity under his watch.

There was a commotion in the bleachers.

Yelling.

Scuffling, and more yelling.

Women screaming.

And then, suddenly, it was all over.

CHAPTER 22

PAUL PULLED BACK the heavy drapes and looked down at the Bellagio's fountains. It was nearly noon and six months to the date when Vivian and Paul had come in one, two at the Four Queens tournament. They had played poker in the Bellagio's nice poker room until one that morning.

Paul looked back at the sleeping Vivian and thought how lucky he was. He had finally been honest with a woman. He was madly in love with her and he felt, whole, fulfilled and really happy for the first time in his life. It was with sadness and a little bit of guilt that he remembered the drive to the airport with Vivian and his subsequent conversation with Maureen after the tournament.

Paul had tipped the valet $25 as the BMW, loaded with lots of luggage and boxes were readied for Vivian's and Paul's departure. "This has been so much fun," Paul said as they pulled out from under the valet area. "And our great poker playing assures us of lots more tournaments. Your being a new millionaire and all makes me want to marry you for your money, not just because I love you so damn much."

"Right now," Vivian said, "I'm thinking the same thing. Marriage! I love you too Paul Langley." She laughed huskily, like the old Vivian.

"By the way," Paul said switching subjects, "that security guy was actually a cop with the Vegas police department. He only worked part time at the Four Queens. He told me, I was right about that Goodwin, fellow. Nuts. He said it wouldn't be long before they got the names of all the gang members as Dee had already given them all the information they need on RJ."

"You really think we're out of danger?" Vivian asked. "Perhaps we should get a gun."

"I've said this before," Paul said as the BMW slid to a stop at a crosswalk. "I believe the Mafia has made him persona non grata, and this was RJ's plan and only his plan. They'll let him hang on his own. No need to get guns, as they won't want or can't have anything to do with this. It's not their style. I don't want anything to happen to you,"

"Oh Paul, I hope you're right," Vivian said. "I'd love to plan a future with you and not worry about him. So you think we'll be safe?"

"I almost guarantee it." Paul tried to say with conviction.

Before arriving at the airport, they went over their stories again, to make sure they were straight. "We'll just answer their questions based on my story," Paul said. "It's the best thing we can do."

"Hang on," Paul told her, turning up the radio. "Listen."

"Also in the headlines today, four men and a player were arrested today after a foiled attempt to rob nearly two million dollars from the Four Queens Hotel and Casino in Downtown Las Vegas. The Four Queens Hotel was hosting the final day of the big stakes poker tournament when Las Vegas Police and hotel security thwarted the attempted robbery. Other gang members are being sought. No injuries were reported. More details after this word."

Paul double-parked next to the entrance of Northwest Airlines. Swiveling her long legs Vivian came into Paul's arms as he opened her door. "Too bad you're wearing slacks," Paul told her. "I'd like to have had another nice 'shot.'

"I can't wait to give you another shot either and I've been thinking about how I'm going to collect on that side bet!" The old Vivian had returned, Paul unloaded her luggage and waved at a Sky Cap. "Call me on my cell phone when you arrive in Chicago. I want to make sure you have arrived safely."

After he left, Paul ticked off in his mind things he had to do in the next half-hour: Get gas, and call Maureen, in that order. Was he going to tell her face-to-face, or on the phone? Somehow finding out what was going on at eNovalon was not that important any longer. He really didn't care how his implementations of software were doing around the country. He had decided on his future, it was clear and bright, and included a vivacious, smart red head.

Driving about 80 mph down highway I-15, he punched in Maureen's number.

"It's Paul," he said when she answered. "I'm on my way back home."

"Oh God Paul, I've been so worried about you. How did it go? You're coming back so soon. I thought you were going to Los Angeles after. You are bringing back bags of money, aren't you? You must have really been busy to not call me at all for the last two days."

"Yes, I've really been busy," he told her. "It was a grueling contest and I had little time to call, I'm sorry." Paul said, knowing that she wouldn't quite believe him.

"Well, I can't wait to hear all about it. When do you get home? I could come over if it's not too late."

"I don't expect to get home until well after midnight," Paul told her. "Perhaps we can meet somewhere for dinner tomorrow night. Somewhere near your house or the office?"

Maureen paused. "Oh I don't like the sound of this. You don't want me to come over. It's only bad news when a man wants to meet somewhere other than his house. What did you do? Meet another woman?"

"Probably this isn't the time to discuss this," he said feeling like a shit, but determined to be honest. "Can we meet, or if you really prefer, you can come over."

"Why don't you call me tomorrow and we'll figure it out," she said in a low voice and something about the way she said it told Paul she that she didn't expect the call.

Paul's big BMW pushed on to Auburn with the sounds of Stan Kenton's "My Old Flame" blasting inside.

"Did you get the paper?" Vivian asked, pulling Paul away from his recollection and his viewing of the Bellagio fountains.

"Yes, it's on the couch, I haven't read it yet."

"Well, RJ's trial starts today I wonder what the paper says."

"I'm sure it's full of the same stuff. I'm so glad we didn't end up having to testify."

"As I told you originally, when I informed them that we must remain anonymous in return for the information I provided, they promised to hold up their part of the bargain."

"I was so worried. I'm still surprised that RJ's attorney didn't ask us any questions or require us to testify."

"It would just provide more proof of his intent to pull this off," Paul said, kissing her forehead. "I'm proud of you. We stuck to our original plan and story."

"Do you think we still need to worry about Dee and what he may say on the stand?

"No way. He'll come across as trying to save his own skin and half crazy. The DA will make him sound ridiculous. Even if he says that somehow I kicked his legs away from the cylinder. Besides they have full confessions from some of RJ's other gang members. Remember how it answered our question as to why we would've had to wait for our split?"

"Oh, yes, I remember," Vivian said. "Their idea was to hide the money in the ceiling of the hotel's kitchen and come back several months later to retrieve it."

Paul remembered the scene after his watch tingled. It was like a good movie, that he would watch repeatedly.

The electric tingling had barley subsided when with his right leg, Paul swept the floor beneath the table.

Contact!

Paul kept moving his leg so powerfully that Dee's legs shifted to the side. Suddenly there was a commotion in the bleachers. Someone yelled and then a woman screamed.

The red-jacketed security man disappeared under the table as a uniformed guard, stepped over the rope, and placed an arm on Dee's shoulder.

There was more commotion from the crowd as additional guards and security men moved into the audience. People scattered. Cameramen pointed their lenses first here and then there, panning the general confusion.

"Let's go back to bed," Vivian said, grinning, putting his 'movie' on hold.

"In a minute," he told her. "I want to read what the paper says."

The Las Vegas Review Journal's Headlines:

Trial starts in Four Queens Heist Attempt

Ex-Mafia Rocco Justini and Five Others Face Jury

Las Vegas, Nevada Prosecutors allege all six defendants, including a player – Dee Goodwin, led by Justini-planned the failed robbery. Three of the would be thieves were armed and face more severe punishment. Federal Prosecutors are also re-opening case of extortion against Justini.

Of all the places to plan a robbery like this; A Las Vegas casino, full of surveillance equipment and alert security staff.

During opening statements, the Clark County prosecutor is expected to outline the entire case against the gang, held without bail, now referred to as the "Dumb Queens Gang." ....

Paul put the paper down. "I'm not going to read any more right now. So Mrs. Langley, are we going to our house site today? They are supposed to be laying the tile."

END

POKER TERMS

A Texas Hold em poker game goes as follows:

1. The betting structure can vary. Sometimes antes are used, but most games start with two players to the left of the dealer placing out a predetermined amount of money so there is an initial amount to get things started. This is called the blinds.

2. The dealer shuffles up a complete deck of 52 playing cards.

3. Each player is dealt two cards face down. These are called your hole or pocket cards.

4. Then there is a round of betting starting with the person to the left of the two who posted the blinds. This round is usually referred to by the term pre-flop.

5. Much like most games of poker, players can check, raise, or fold.

6. After the betting round ends, the dealer discards the top card of the deck. This is called a burn card. This is done to prevent cheating.

7. The dealer then flips the next three cards face up on the table. These cards are called the flop. These are community cards that anyone can use in combination with their two pocket cards to form a poker hand.

8. There is another round of betting starting with the player to the left of the dealer.

9. After the betting concludes, the dealer burns another card and flips one more onto the table. This is called the turn card, or River. Players can use this sixth card now to form a five-card poker hand.

10. The player to the left of the dealer begins another round of betting. In many types of games, this is where the bet size doubles.

11. Finally, the dealer burns a card and places a final card face up on the table. This is called the river or Fifth Street. Players can now use any of the five cards on the table or the two cards in their pocket to form a five-card poker hand.

12. There is one final round of betting starting with the player to the left of the dealer.

13. After that, all of the players remaining in the game begin to

reveal their hands. This begins with the player to the left of the last player to call. It's called the showdown.

14. The player who shows the best hand wins! There are cases where players with equal hands share the winnings.

Some other terms used in no-limit Texas Hold'em.

1. **All-in** - Also known as **Going All-in**. To bet all your chips, or to call with all your chips. If another player bets more chips than you have in a No Limit game, you can go all-in and stake your total stack against an equivalent amount of your opponent's stack.

2. **Big Blind** The larger of the two forced bets preflop. The person in second position posts the big blind, which is equivalent to a small bet.

3. **Small Blind** The smaller of the two forced bets preflop. The person in first position posts the small blind, which is equivalent to half of a small bet.

4. **Preflop** The stage of a Hold'em game when you have two cards in your hand and there are no cards on the board yet.

5. **Gutshot** Also known as **Belly Buster**. An inside straight draw. An example of a gutshot (also known as belly buster) is to have 89JQ, aiming to hit a ten.

6. **Flop** The first three board cards in Hold'em.

7. **Offsuit** Also known as: **Unsuited.** A Hold'em starting hand with two cards of different suits. These hands

are weaker than suited hands because of fewer flush possibilities.

8. **Nut Flush** – The highest possible flush hand.

9. **Slowplay or Slowraise**. Slowplaying is a deceptive move. It is the opposite of bluffing. It means to check or bet weakly when one holds a strong hand. The point of the slowplay is so the competition builds a hand that will become the second best hand. Then, when the competition builds this hand, one will jam the pot with bets.

10. **WSOP** World Series of Poker

Howard Jenkins has had a varied career, in corporate America performing senior executive management of procurement, contract administration, manufacturing, and information technology in industries as varied as Aerospace and Defense, commercial aircraft manufacturing, software and the restaurant business. Career changes moved him from California, to Puerto Rico, to Minnesota, to Arizona, to Kansas, to Colorado and finally to Las Vegas. A willing and capable public speaker, Jenkins has written several columns for Hospitality Technology Magazine as well as several corporate position papers and major project management "how-to" manuals. Jenkins retired from corporate life in early 2004 to follow his dream of writing novels. His first book, *The Big Deal* to some extent follows the writing advice, "write about what you know."

Born in Harrow, England during the London 'blitz,' his parents immigrated to the US when Howard was just five shortly after the war. He, his older sister, and younger brother were quickly immersed into the culture of Southern California, but their parents reminded them of their English/Welsh heritage on a daily basis.

Howard has two sons, and a daughter, arriving when he was very young, and two grandchildren all in California. His new grown stepson lives in Arizona. Howard, married in October 2005, to the former Lynda Schaefer on their tenth happy anniversary of their original meeting. Lynda and Howard love Las Vegas.

Jenkins, in addition to writing, listening to jazz, and gambling, volunteers his time with the Las Vegas Metropolitan Police Department helping in the Crime Prevention area and Handicap Parking enforcement.

Printed in the United States
86902LV00006B/17/A

9 781434 323941